STAKE SAUCE

STAKE SAUCE, ARC 1: The Secret Ingredient is Love. No, Really.
Copyright © 2017 by RoAnna Sylver.

Published by The Kraken Collective.
www.krakencollectivebooks.com

Cover art by RoAnna Sylver.
Interior design by Lyssa Chiavari.
Tarot illustrations by Noel Heimpel.
Typefaces by Misprinted Type.

This is a work of fiction. Names, characters, places, and incidents either are the product of the author's imagination or are used fictitiously. Any resemblance to actual events, locales, organizations, or persons, living or dead, is entirely coincidental and beyond the intent of the author.

All rights reserved, which includes the right to reproduce this book or portions thereof in any form whatsoever except as provided by the U.S. Copyright Law.

To my family

especially my small snorking friend who has about eight teeth, and no fangs. ♥

STAKE SAUCE

A MODULATING FREQUENCIES SERIES

Arc 1: The Secret Ingredient is Love (No, Really.)

ROANNA SYLVER

Kraken Collective

Dramatis Personae

JUDE MILTON: Used To Jump Out Of Helicopters To Fight Fires. Mall Cop By Day, Vampire Hunter By Night, Vigilance Always. Don't Say "Hey."

PIXIE: An Unsuccessful Vampire and Even Less Successful Musician. Punk Isn't Dead! He Is. That Doesn't Mean He Goes Around Biting People, Come On. Gross.

EVA CORONA: Mall Superintendent And Productive Member Of Society. Just Wants To Get Through A Day Without Losing Another Coffee. Or Friend.

JASPER: Chases Away Memories And Nightmares With Rare Books And Records; None For Sale. Has A Persona For Every Day Of The Week. Can't Remember The Real One.

FELIX: Search And Rescue Medic Who Couldn't Be Rescued, But May Yet Be Found. Greatly Mourned, Missed and Maligned.

NAILS: Sharpest Claws And Strategic Skills This Side Of The Veil. Dreamed Of Gold-Paved Streets. Got Her Wish.

MAESTRA: A Virtuosic Artist On A Skateboard And Anywhere Else. Born For The Spotlight. Died For It, Too.

THE WITCH: Mysterious and Very Cool Benefactor and Mostly-Knowing, Little-Saying Seer. Will Cast Eldritch Magics For Coffee. Wears Shades At Night. Suspicious.

Cruce: A Charismatic but Vicious Underworld Predator. Bite Even Worse Than His Bark.

And Finally, Just Offstage But Never Far From The Spotlight: A Man Of Wealth And Taste, Whose Name We Don't Have To Guess.

STAKE SAUCE

THE SECRET INGREDIENT IS LOVE.
(NO, REALLY.)

✸ XV THE DEVIL ✸

ACT ONE:
Going Through the Motions

"ALL RIGHT." Eva Corona rested her folded hands on an uncompleted incident report form, steadily looking across her desk. A pen sat beside the papers, but she didn't yet pick it up. "Who was it this time?"

"The usual suspects," said the pale, thin man on the other side of the desk. He wore a blue security guard's uniform and stood at attention, back ramrod-straight. Aside from speaking, he held perfectly still, grey eyes fixed on her.

"Okay." Eva gave a half-nod, tilting her head. "So, teenagers?"

"Two of them."

"And you said they were 'the usual suspects.'"

"That's right."

"Refresh my memory?" When he didn't respond immediately, she gave a moderately exasperated sigh. Pulling teeth, like always. "At ease, soldier."

As if unused to the motion, Jude Milton rolled his shoulders and made himself relax. But he couldn't seem to keep it up for long and shifted into something like a military at-ease position, clasping his hands firmly behind his back.

"I didn't mean literally…" Eva said, then opted for a less-resistant path and let it go. This conversation was going to be hard enough already. "Never mind. So. Two of them?"

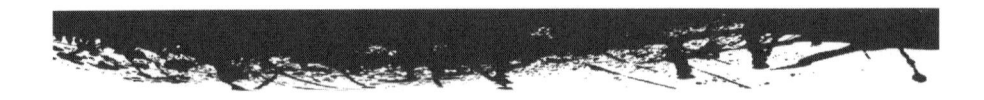

"One was on a skateboard," he said haltingly, in a quiet and raspy voice that suggested he might need to clear his throat. She wondered if this was the first time he spoke today. Sounded like it. "The other wore those shoes. With the wheels."

"Heelys?"

"Inside. And down the center of the escalator." He sounded almost offended, but didn't break his steady gaze. Her eyebrows came together in an expression of hesitant scrutiny. He said nothing, just waited for her next question.

"So, any description besides their wheels?"

"They were... pale." Even—technically—at ease, Jude fidgeted under her gaze, his eyes dropping briefly to her desk and the still-blank incident report form.

Eva hesitated, prolonging the tense silence like she was locked in a chess game and running out of moves. It wasn't that Jude was going to win— neither of them ever came out of these talks a winner. But she could feel something building like far-off thunder. Familiar thunder, ominous. But like a parched traveler whose only oasis lay across an active minefield, she grit her teeth and kept moving. "How pale are we talking about? Are you saying they were white kids?"

"No," he said, then corrected himself, continuing in a neutral, matter-of-fact near-monotone. "Sort of. One was. The other, I believe, was African American. She had the skateboard."

"Okay." Now Eva picked up the form and clicked her pen top, trying to fill the damn thing out fast, before he could say anything else. "So, black girl on a skateboard, white kid in heel—"

"Grey kids."

She stopped writing. Held perfectly still, as if that would somehow postpone the inevitable. "No."

"Skateboard kid was a kind of slate grey-ish—"

"Jude, *no*."

"And her friend was paler, but still definitely grey, no pigment at all." His words started to speed up, but he didn't raise his voice from its plain, inexpressive neutral. "Probably because they don't have any oxygen left in their red blood cells. Which aren't actually red anymore. My theory is that the shift from living to reanimated bodily fluids and deoxygenation affects skin coloration as well as blood—they don't bleed, that's why they drink it—or it has something to do with necrotizing-but-preserved flesh. Whatever the case, they definitely—"

"Oh my God," Eva sighed, pinching the bridge of her nose—then immediately stopping, because the motion scrunched the Band-Aid plastered over it, one a pink color about four shades too light for her deep brown skin. It was almost coming off already because of the number of times she'd performed that particular gesture today, and yet, it still wasn't the most annoying thing in the room. "Anything else out of the ordinary? Anything I can actually write down here?"

His brow furrowed, as if he were replaying whatever he'd seen over in his head and not liking a second of it. "No. These are definitely the same ones I've seen around here the past several weeks. They have to have a lair somewhere nearby."

"A lair. All right." Eva clicked the pen closed again and let it drop. She leaned back in her cushioned leather chair and stared up at the ceiling. She'd seen burning buildings that weren't as big of disasters as this conversation. "Thank you. Really appreciate you reporting in today, Jude, always a pleasure."

"I can give a much more detailed description if you need one, Ma'am." He paused. "If you'll accept it."

"Now I'm 'Ma'am.'" She went to pinch the bridge of her nose again, remembered the damn Band-Aid and residual ache just in time, and covered her eyes briefly instead. "You're mad at me. You're passive-aggressive and you're mad at me."

"Just doing my job. Ma'am."

She rolled her eyes, then took the opportunity to give him a good hard look for the first time since he'd set foot in her office. Jude's face was always drawn and pale, almost an unhealthy grey himself. This morning, and not for the first time, she'd told some other mall security guards off for unfavorably comparing him to one of the living dead he calmly but relentlessly insisted walked among them. She'd never admit it, or let anyone run their mouths like that without an ass-kicking, but the jerks had a point.

These days, Jude looked a little more dead than alive. Especially around the eyes, with the deep, dark circles underneath. His tendency to stare—into space, directly at people, or through them, as if he'd forgotten they were there—didn't help either. Today his eyes were so blank, and his tone so deadpan, she couldn't tell if he was serious or sarcastic. Any other day she might not mind his characteristic reticence, but today...

"Just doing your job? I don't think so. You're going a little above and beyond. See this?" Eva gestured to the 'flesh'-colored Band-Aid across her nose. "My day hasn't been sunshine and rainbows either. Know what happened this morning, the second I set foot in here?"

Jude stayed quiet, seeming to know he was about to hear the answer anyway.

"I'm walking," Eva reflected. "Coffee. Favorite shirt. Bluebirds in the parking lot, just a real nice morning. That kid with the purple hair from The Abyss down the far end waves at me. Jasper's just opening up his place, we say hi. He acts like he's up to no good, and I'm catching him in the act, but he's messing with me, you know how he does. It almost feels normal. Then, out of the corner of my eye, I see one of them."

"One of..." Jude's eyes lit up a little, but he—wisely—caught himself and shut his mouth as she watched. Progress.

"This skinny, ratty-looking little punk comes sashaying out of the food court and wings a crumpled-up burger wrapper at my latte. Except I don't know it's paper, I think it's a damn baseball, 'cause first he winds up like it's the World Series!"

Jude stayed quiet. To his credit, he didn't smile, he maintained eye contact, and at least seemed to be listening. But it didn't matter how genuine he seemed if nothing actually improved. The longer they knew one another, the less she seemed to know him. But he was going to learn something today, she resolved. Whether he liked it or not.

"I see what he's gonna do, and I got two seconds to decide what to protect. Coffee, shirt, face, I'm trying to save three things with two hands, when—bam!" She mimed something flying at her face, then 'exploded' her fist, spreading her fingers wide before dropping her hand to the desk. "Ball hits face."

"He hurt your nose?" Jude asked, now at least sounding concerned.

"It was paper, Jude. No, I'm so shocked, I try to block with my coffee hand…" She let out an embarrassed laugh, waving at the Band-Aid across her nose. Almost forgot it wasn't five years ago, and she wasn't telling her friend a tragic story just to vent. "I hit my own nose with the thermos. Which they both saw—Jasper and the goth kid, who was nice enough to get me some ice."

"I'm sorry," Jude said, and the too-rare smile he gave her in return wasn't gloating or mocking—she'd never actually seen that on his face. He looked sheepish enough that she wondered if he remembered doing something similarly embarrassing and just never mentioned it, the way they never really talked anymore.

"Me too," she said, shaking her head and trying to hold onto the moment. Stay connected, if only for a few seconds. "I'm just glad I went with iced this morning."

"You want me to keep an eye out? I think I know the guy you mean." Jude actually sounded more engaged now. But he was too late in several ways.

"I'd rather you were there when I called security." Eva's smile faded as she returned to the present. Their shared past and disconnected present weighed her down like a backpack full of bricks. She wasn't angry anymore. Anger required energy, and hers was in increasingly short supply. "But you weren't."

"I'm sorry," he said again, but without the smile this time. His eyes flicked away. Not for the first time, Eva wondered what the hell happened to her friend, the man she'd trusted with her life too many times to count. Granted, the past five years had been full of changes for all three of them—her, Jude, and Jasper, all starting a new life together—and not nearly enough of those changes were good. Still, Eva thought her transition from the fire engine to the desk had been relatively smooth. Jasper had to miss the excitement and drama, but he appreciated the normalcy too, she knew. Jude, on the other hand, seemed... not just a different person. He didn't even seem here at all.

"Where were you?" Eva asked, the question aimed at the Jude of the last five years as much as the one in front of her. Again, she hoped and prayed he'd have a good answer, instead of the one she expected. Maybe he'd been occupied with a shoplifter. Maybe there'd been some parking-lot scuffle to break up. In all their time here, she couldn't remember any serious crises, but messy nonsense still happened day-to-day. After five years of increasingly-disappointing predictability, it was getting harder to give Jude the benefit of the doubt.

"I was..." He stared down at the incident report paper. He wasn't standing 'at ease' anymore, thin shoulders dropping a little. "I'll be there next time."

"Glad to hear it," she said, but didn't feel very happy. Or convinced. She was even less encouraged by the suddenly thoughtful look on his face. "What?"

Jude paused, looking like he was trying to decide how much to say or reveal. Once, they'd told each other everything without a second thought. The difference hurt. So did the distance. "It was just one guy, right?"

"Yeah, just the one. Skinny ginger-looking kid, teenage or maybe a little older, hard to tell with objects flying at my face. Why?"

"The ones I keep running into are two girls," he said, actually sounding relieved. And still convinced, Eva realized with some dismay. She didn't know which was worse, Jude making up wild stories that tested her trust and friendship, or Jude actually believing what he was saying. "Never seen any with that description. It's probably fine."

"It's not fine," she said bluntly, feeling a small flare of something like annoyance, but much more personal, more painful. Betrayal. "Someone threw something at me, and ran away while I stood there drenched in iced coffee with a bloody nose. Which you would have seen, if you were there when I needed you."

"I'll..." He started, then stopped. She waited, but he said nothing.

"Jude, we've been doing this dance for five years. Isn't it time we talked about something else?"

"I know what I saw," he said in a low, steady voice. "And you already know what I'm going to say."

"You've stuck to your story, I've gotta give you that." Eva shrugged, sighed, and resigned herself to one more dance.

"That's because it's the truth."

She shut her eyes. Of all things, that was one she never wanted to hear. "I don't know what to believe, Jude. You come in here and tell me that Portland—and the Sunrise Plaza Mall, specifically—is infested with undead, bloodsucking pests? Actual vampires preying on people who go down the wrong street at night? And that five years ago..." She trailed off and let the silence hang. She didn't have the words to fill it.

Jude took a small step forward for the first time, reaching out to gingerly touch the desk between them with two fingers. "Believe that I wouldn't lie to you. Not after all this."

"I don't think you're lying," she said, hating the uncertainty in her own voice. She hated all of this. "Not... not exactly."

"Believe that I'm dedicated to protecting this place, and the people in it, from threats of all kinds." He sounded so sure. She wished she could borrow some of that certainty.

"I want to believe that," she said, certain of this at least. "That you'd still walk through fire to save someone in danger. That's why I wanted you for this job." She smiled down at his faint reflection in her desk's glossy surface. "Because the fire's still in you. And knowing you're here gives me a chance to rest easy."

"I can't rest easy." It sounded like a resolution, almost a promise, and it was the most familiar thing she'd heard this whole strange day. It sounded like the old Jude, the one she knew five years ago. The only Jude she recognized. It almost hurt. "Not if my company leader doesn't trust me. That's on me, not you. I'll do better."

"Jude." She took a deep breath and let it out slowly. "First of all, I am not your company leader anymore. I'm a mall superintendent, and you're a mall cop. You're here to keep an eye out for rowdy kids, shoplifters, and to call the actual authorities if someone throws anything more dangerous than a ball of trash... and I'm here to sit behind a desk, push papers, and keep the lights on." She smiled, and it was tired but ultimately satisfied. "Do you know how long I've wanted a desk job?"

"A long time," he said softly. "You deserve a rest."

"We all do. This is the easy life, my guy. We made it. You, me, and Jasper—whatever the hell else he gets up to, he's here and doing better, that's what matters. Practically retirement, except we still get to see each other every day. I call that winning. It's more than a lot of people get."

"I know," Jude said, sounding so serious and earnest she felt a flicker of hope deep down, that maybe they weren't as estranged as it seemed; maybe they could still come back from this. But she knew better by now than to jump at that kind of faint hope. She didn't usually like where she landed. "It's more than Felix got. And he wouldn't want me to throw it all away."

Some words still hit like the proverbial ton of bricks. Some names. After five years, she could hear and say Felix's name without a wave of nausea or cold weight in her stomach—but that was when she was ready for it. Out of everything, she hadn't expected Jude to bring up that name in particular, and that knocked her too off-balance to ignore. Her smile faded along with the last of her energy. "No, he wouldn't. We're the lucky ones, Jude. Enjoy it. For everyone who can't."

"Anything else... Eva?" His voice was still quiet. Some of the tension had finally faded from his body, but it just left him looking tired.

"No." She shook her head, looking again at the dark circles under his eyes and wondering if her own matched. "Go home. Go home and *rest*," she specified, knowing what would happen if she didn't. "No more chasing shadows for you. Not tonight."

"Good night," he said, giving her what she suspected was an attempted smile. She appreciated the effort, it was getting harder for both of them.

"See you tomorrow." Eva tried to smile back, but didn't succeed any more than he had. How strange it was to miss someone when they were standing right in front of you.

Jude turned on his heel and strode out of the room, and Eva sank back into her chair, suddenly exhausted. As she watched her friend leave, she wasn't entirely sure whether to laugh at the absurdity—vampires in the mall, he says—or cry for everything they'd been and everything they'd lost. A few seconds after the door closed, Eva put her forehead down on her desk. But first she ripped the rumpled Band-Aid off her nose.

🔥

The night outside was damp and cool. It had just rained—it was Oregon, of course it had—and even the night air of the parking lot smelled fresh and clean. Jude's eyes flicked into the darkest shadows as he walked the unfamiliar path, automatically scanning ahead for escapes and dead ends. He counted steps toward alleys and parked cars, paused just before rounding a corner or object large enough for a predator—living or otherwise—to hide behind.

It wasn't his usual route home—he didn't want to risk running into Eva again as she made her own way back to their apartment building. Being off the clock helped both of their respective stress levels and she'd be friendly to him, he knew, even after their sort-of-fight about punk kids and coffee malfunctions—and him not being there when she needed him. At one time, that would have been unthinkable. He'd failed her today, yes. But the risk was calculated and the stakes were higher than either one of them alone.

And Eva wasn't nearly as well-adjusted and together as she liked to think. The flash of pain in her eyes when he'd dropped the bomb, the name 'Felix,' always on their minds and hardly ever on their lips... he almost regretted it, but her reaction only strengthened his resolve. She had to know what drove Jude's every waking thought—the same thing that drove her, really. Eva just didn't know it yet. She wouldn't hear it. And given the choice between an awkward conversation and facing a night full of potential horrors, Jude knew what he'd pick every time.

He almost made it to the far side of the lot before he saw them. A pair of figures near a streetlamp, just outside its pale yellow circle of light.

"You kids shouldn't be out this late," he called, taking a few steps toward them. The streetlight flickered above. Maybe they were here for some of Jasper's less-than-legal substances and/or services that he and Eva never quite got around to checking on. Maybe they were just bored. It didn't matter. His job was to protect them all.

"It's getting dark," Jude tried again, and didn't get an answer. The pale light sputtered and went out. The darkness was complete, and so was the silence. A chill rushed up his spine and he almost kept moving, faster this time. But he stayed where he was, because they couldn't have left either, not without making some noise. "Listen, it's not safe—"

The light came back on, bright as a white-hot spotlight on a stage. The two kids were gone. In their place were monsters.

Their eyes flashed an iridescent blue-green with thin, vertical pupils. Like cats, Jude thought wildly. Black, leathery wings rose behind them, spanning four or five feet on either side, partly blocking out the bright light.

The short one was a very pale grey, with spiky, short blonde hair and small, long-fingered hands outstretched toward him and flashing lethal-looking claws. Toes as well, he realized. They'd ditched their shoes, heelys and otherwise, and now the claws on the ends of their talon-like toes flashed through the air as well. The taller one was a darker grey, the tight curls of her black hair falling all the way down to her waist in meticulously neat coils.

When she struck a dramatic pose in the spotlight and waved her long arms, the streetlamp's light flickered again, but this time it intensified.

High-pitched keening erupted from two wide-stretched mouths, an alien sound. Choking, Jude bent over almost double, fists defensively blocking his face. As he staggered back, he caught another glance at the creatures' faces—and realized the terrifying expressions were smiles. They were laughing at him. Their grin-bared teeth flashed along with their eyes, very bright, and very sharp.

Jude froze, and the world along with him. He couldn't breathe.

It was five years ago and fire blazed all around. The night wind wasn't cool and damp anymore. Instead, superheated air seared his lungs when he inhaled. Screams cut through the dark as helicopter blades thrummed in the distance, getting closer. Not fast enough, help would never reach them in time. Static crackled in his ear. His throat was raw from yelling for help—*where was Felix? Was he all right?*—and breathing in smoke, but the radio didn't work. That had been the first thing to go. The smell of blood was so thick in the air he almost gagged, metallic sting sharp in his nostrils and mouth.

The moon was full and very bright. Like the streetlight. Like reflective eyes. Like teeth.

Running hadn't worked then and it wouldn't now, Jude knew that deep in his bones. He'd never seen anything move as fast as the thing that had swept by him that night, leaving death in its wake. He couldn't fight back and hope to survive, either. But at least he'd go down with his fists up, standing between the creatures and the mall lights behind him. He'd end the way he started, protecting Eva, Jasper, and everything good left in the world.

Head down and arms up, Jude waited for the death blow. It didn't come.

Slowly, he lowered his hands and looked up, eyes wide and unblinking, frozen like a deer caught in the last headlights it would see on this Earth. He saw the flashes of two grins, the same laughing faces with razor-toothed smiles—but somehow, the tilt of their heads looked perplexed, and their smiles confused. They didn't attack. The two creatures just stared at him for a few seconds, looking almost awkward, as if they'd just told a joke that had flown over his head.

They turned away from him to face one another and actually held a whispered conversation. He couldn't hear what they said, but it didn't sound like the guttural growls he expected. More like a whispered exchanged between girls giggling in the food court. The familiarity was as disorienting as the strangeness, paralyzing in itself.

Then the shorter of the two waved the taller one away, shaking her head. She turned on her clawed foot and took a few short-legged but powerful strides, then launched herself into the air on quick-spreading, dark wings. Her companion followed after shooting one last, almost pitying look back at the terrified, motionless human huddled on the ground below.

Jude stayed there long after the sky was clear. Then, cursing himself for his own helplessness, he scrambled to his feet and ran the rest of the way home.

The Sunset Towers building was an even more welcome sight than usual. Jude slipped into apartment number 359 and immediately locked the door behind him, then fell against it, trying to slow his panicked breathing. Cold sweat made his blue uniform shirt cling to his skin. He'd felt a chill the second he saw those four glowing eyes. Gasping, he rubbed his clammy face with both hands, running his fingers through his usually-neat, now-disheveled, straight black hair.

Real. They were real. They'd been there, in the parking lot. Flashing eyes, gleaming fangs, bright, sharp grins. Staring right at him. But they hadn't attacked—why? No. Not important. What mattered was that he wasn't seeing things. He still had his grip on reality.

He thought. He hoped. Wasn't the very nature of hallucinations that they fooled the senses? You saw things that weren't—

No, dammit. Couldn't start thinking like that. Not after the case he'd made to Eva. Not after the closest encounter he'd had since that last traumatic, life-defining, threshold-crossing night five years ago. Jude had only caught glimpses ever since. But he'd told her the truth. He'd been telling the truth night after night, he'd never lied once and his senses weren't lying to him now.

He knew what he saw.

But they were gone now, and he had no chance of catching them. He hadn't even tried. He'd panicked, almost collapsed with helpless terror. Couldn't tell Eva. She wouldn't want to hear, she'd reject it out of self-preservation, anyone would. Not that he blamed her. She was right. They'd put their own lives on the line more times than he could count, for innocent people and each other. Eva had done it more than once for him. She'd earned her rest and reward a thousand times over and if she wanted a boring, safe desk job, that's what she got. He owed her that much and more.

Jude sank down onto his old, faded sofa, and it made a noise like a weary sigh. So did Jude. Everything hurt. Old, familiar pain, muscles and joints aching down to his core. He felt hollow, and cold as if he'd swallowed ice that refused to melt in his stomach.

He had his share of scars, visible and otherwise. Not as many burns as one might expect. Most of them were from impacts or lacerations, protective suits couldn't eliminate those entirely. Occupational hazards, and most of them were long since healed. Likewise for his chest. His now-faded top surgery scars had been entirely voluntary, and carried an even greater sense of pride than his other physical reminders. Scars meant he survived, and none of them really bothered him anymore.

But his left leg did. As always, pain radiated from his toes to midway up his thigh in degrees, a slow burn that started whenever he pushed past his limits—which he did, consistently, ignoring it until he couldn't anymore. Then the pain grew to a regular throb of agony, until there was no pause between the beats. After nights like this, the whole thing just became pain.

He let out another sound that was less a sigh and more a half-stifled groan as he sat up, then leaned forward to roll up his left pants leg. There was no reason for his entire leg to hurt, even though the scarring—gashes, not burns, stretching from his knee to his thigh—had taken years to fully heal. That thick layer of scar tissue was never going away. But the pain in his shin and foot shouldn't exist at all.

No nerve endings in a prosthetic leg. It didn't make sense to his logical brain. Of course, a lot of things didn't make sense anymore, phantom limb pain most of all.

It didn't sound real until you lived it, something gone that you could still feel. And no amount of psychoanalysis or technical medical knowledge (still-active neural connections no longer attached to anything, still doing what they were designed to do, registering pain, particularly when triggered by associated traumatic memories) made a difference. Nothing made it stop.

But he could start to ease his leg off and try to convince his body that there was no need for this. Get ready for bed and try to relax, even though he'd been trying desperately to relax for five years. Jude usually only fell asleep when he couldn't keep his eyes open another second. But like with everything else, he'd keep trying.

BANG.

Jude threw himself to the floor, flinging his arms up over his head. Something had hit the window, almost shattering it. They'd found him. He readjusted his prosthetic and army-crawled to the kitchen where he kept his more extreme measures, finding some grim satisfaction in the fact that he'd *told* everyone it would end like this.

Sometimes, constant hypervigilance was a blessing. Instinct and muscle memory had saved Jude's life more times than he could count and it would again. He didn't even have to look to find the drawer where he kept his weapons. When he stood, he held a small vial of consecrated holy water. At least, consecrated and blessed according to Jasper's assured expertise and guarantee. If that guarantee didn't live up to the hype, Jude would have words for him. But then, unless it did, he wouldn't get the chance.

Jude took a deep breath and tried once again to steady his nerves. It didn't really work, but he still shut his eyes and counted silently down. *Three, two...*

On *one*, he jumped in front of the window, eyes wide open, teeth bared, holy water raised, ready to spray it at the…bedraggled little bat flopping around on the windowsill outside.

Its scruffy fur stuck up in clumps and actually looked pink. Maybe this particularly unlucky bat had flown into some wet paint, just like it must have flown into the window and banged its head, too dazed to take off again. The little thing did look sad and confused, wiggling its big ears and turning its fuzzy pink head like it was trying to figure out where it was and what to do next. Jude knew the feeling.

Exhausted again, he lowered his weapons. Just a bat. His paranoia really was at an all-time high, but that wasn't surprising after the night he'd had. No wonder he was jumping at shadows, noises, and bats. Maybe he was even seeing things. But this seemed real enough, even if he couldn't remember ever seeing a bat this close before, especially not a pink—

BANG.

Jude jumped again, this time nearly out of his clammy skin. His heart slammed in his chest and his head spun from the sheer adrenaline. Until he realized the noise wasn't actually another impact, it was more like…

Knock-knock-knock.

Jude flopped back against the wall, almost collapsing in a weak heap for the second time that night. After a few seconds of shaky-kneed relief, he made himself focus on the apartment door and how to actually open it. Nightmarish creatures of the darkness were unlikely to knock. And wasn't there something about them needing to be invited in? Jude didn't even like inviting other humans in.

So, silently and smoothly, he set about undoing every lock. He had seven: the standard lock and bolt chain, two more keyed, and three deadbolts. Non-regulation, probably breaking several lease rules, but this was one case where rule-following came *after* staying alive. Then, just as quietly, he opened the door a crack to peer out. Jude held his breath, ready to fight for his life or go down swinging.

"Hey Ju—hello," Eva corrected herself, for which he was immediately grateful. Ever since deciding on his name, he'd barely gone a day without someone making a crack about that damn song, every time thinking they were fresh and original. They never were. There was only one person in the world Jude had ever let get away with that and he had no plans to increase that number. Even Eva wasn't allowed, and she always caught herself when the words popped out accidentally. One of many reasons she was one of two remaining people he was ever actually glad to see. Now, she squinted at him through the small gap between the door and the frame, and Jude could just see that she held something—a large pizza box and a bottle. Her Band-Aid was gone, though her nose definitely looked scabbed and bruised. "Uh, I was in the neighborhood, and thought I'd—"

"Oh, thank God." He let out his breath in a rush along with all of his coiled-spring tension, shoulders falling and hands dropping down to his sides. Jude opened the door the rest of the way and glanced up and down the empty hall.

"Hi there," Eva said in a deliberately casual kind of way. "You expecting someone?"

"Huh?" He jumped slightly before somewhat-successfully shoving aside his lingering paranoia and focusing on her. "No. Why do you ask?"

"No reason." Her eyes flicked down to his white-knuckled fists. "What is that?"

"Oh. This?" He glanced down as well and saw he'd forgotten he still had the holy water. "That's nothing. I was just..."

"Okay," she said when he didn't even try to finish the sentence. "Got a minute to talk? Without the spray bottle?"

"Yeah, come on in," he said, waving her in with one hand before realizing it held the holy water and hastily lowering it again. "Um, I can explain this."

"You really don't have to." Once inside, Eva eyed the several locks, actually giving an approving nod. "Got something like this on mine."

"Uh-huh." He was busy peering out the peephole, checking the hallway outside for wings and fangs, and only half-heard.

"Which you're always welcome to stop by and see."

He didn't even answer that time.

"Anyway," Eva rolled her eyes, turning and setting the pizza box down on the counter. She opened and closed the lid a couple of times, wafting the aroma across the room. Then smiled as Jude sniffed and turned around. "Hi. Got your attention now?"

"Pizza?" His eyes widened and mouth dropped open a little.

"Yeah. People eat it for nutrition and pleasure." She took out a slice and held it up, letting the cheese drip. "And steak sauce. From my sister's restaurant, The Pit? Goes real good with the crust."

"Thanks. Thank you," he said a little faintly, shutting the holy water back in its drawer. "You didn't have to do this."

"Did you eat today?"

"Huh?" He looked up, mouth full. His stomach made a soft anticipatory growl as he realized he didn't know the answer to that question.

Eva just chewed while his brain hurried to catch up with his taste buds.

"Oh." Jude swallowed and cleared his throat. "I knew I forgot to do something."

"Thought so." She headed over to the sofa and sank down, letting out a soft sigh that told Jude she was every bit as exhausted as he was.

"Not your job to take care of me, Eva," he said, grabbing a slice and shaking out some of the spicy-smelling red sauce onto his plate.

"There are a lot of things I could say here," she returned quietly, giving him a steady stare. "But we're off the clock. So I'm just going to say I'm sorry for how we left things earlier. I don't like being the bitch, Jude. Believe it or not, I want us all to have the best lives as we can. If Jasper ever graduated from low-key shady shit to actual trouble? You'd better believe I'd shake some sense into him too."

"You're not a bitch, you're the chief." Jude had been busying himself with his food, but now he met her eyes. "And you were right. I've been letting… personal issues get in the way of my job. I'll do better."

"Well, okay." Eva blinked, looking pleasantly surprised. "Glad to hear it. You know I'm gonna hold you to that. Sucks, but I have to."

"Didn't always suck," Jude smiled just a little as he headed over to join her on the couch Not all memories were traumatic. Some of them were still fresh and warm after all this time, and those would live forever. "I just liked it better when you were telling me it was time to jump."

"It was exciting, that's for sure. We did good work." She paused, eyes drifting off into the same kind of faraway haze he found himself caught in more and more. "Still, I wouldn't look back. Not for a second. There's nothing back there for any of us."

"I hear you." He took another bite of pizza, his head slowly clearing and exhaustion fading. "Anyway, I meant what I said, about doing better. No more running around in dark alleys. Not anymore. That's not the life I want."

Yesterday this would have been a lie. An hour ago this would have been a lie. But after tonight, after the parking lot, it wasn't. Jude had spent years chasing shadows. But actually catching up to them, looking into coldly alien faces, unable to move under their stares…

Eva hesitated, looking like she was thinking several more things she was too polite to say. "Is that why you answered the door with the implement of destruction?"

Jude glanced back at the drawer where his holy water awaited the next nocturnal invasion. He couldn't bring himself to be embarrassed by its presence, only reassured. "You can never be too careful."

"Well, in this case I'd say that's about right," she said, eyeing the several locks and deadbolts. "The freaks sure do come out at night. And people do disappear. Like that kid from a couple floors up? The one with the punk haircut, loud music all night?"

Jude swallowed his bite of pizza, frowning, but not at the memory. That particular upstairs neighbor, directly above Jude's apartment and below Eva's, had been a bass-thumping, wall-vibrating thorn in his side for months. But at her words, just-as-loud alarm bells went off in Jude's head now. "He's gone?"

Eva's smile faded as she looked at what had to be his increasingly-disturbed expression. "Yeah. About a month ago. Just never came back one night. Guess they're finally cleaning out his stuff, saw it on the way down."

"Huh." Jude was quiet for a few seconds, trying to mask his growing unease with a neutral, unreadable pokerface. "I thought it was quiet around here."

"Yeah. Wonder if that's how somebody noticed he was missing." Eva might have been half-joking, but she just looked troubled.

"Nobody knows what happened?" Jude leaned forward, resting his elbows on his knees, interest piqued despite himself. He had no desire to start another round, but if he ignored warning signs like this, he'd only have himself to blame when... "Any signs of...?"

"Foul play?" Eva raised her eyebrows, then shrugged. "Nah. Not that I heard, anyway. Guy just disappeared. Like how people disappear every day. I j—" She started to say something else, then shut her mouth and just looked at Jude with a wan expression he was starting to know too well.

"You don't have to worry about me," he said in what he hoped was a comforting tone, but probably not nearly as convincing as he'd have liked.

"Yeah, but I'm gonna." She set down her empty plate and folded her arms, shifting in the deep sofa cushions to look at him straight-on. "Until you give me a reason not to."

He tried to smile. It wasn't easy. He was out of practice. "There's no—"

"Jude."

"I admit," he said slowly, abandoning the attempted smile with some relief. "I might be feeling a small, minor bit of... strain."

"Minor strain?" She stared at him, looking so incredulous it crossed over into amusement.

"It's nothing I can't handle," he asserted. She didn't look convinced, and he couldn't blame her—but he gave a decisive nod anyway. "I'm handling it."

Eva took a deep breath in which he could feel her tension rebuilding. "Jude, I got you this job because I knew you'd be good at it. I wanted someone around I could trust. And before that..." She hesitated one more time. Jude remembered the way his breath used to catch the moment before a dive, stepping through a plane or helicopter's doors and falling toward flames. She was going through the same thing now, the lead-up and the plunge. He'd always recognize the process, and respect it, even if it hurt to watch. Even if some things hurt to hear. "I kept my mouth shut when you said it was monsters that ripped our crew to shreds that night."

"One. There was only one monster," he said very quietly. He shuddered under a wave of vertigo, fighting to keep his equilibrium.

"We fought fires," she said, steadily meeting his gaze until he sighed and leaned back, staring up at his white plaster ceiling. "Not vampires. Not even people. But it was just as dangerous, and I was a hundred feet in the air half the time. We could've died a million different ways, but fangs wasn't one of them."

"I know what I saw," he said, just as quietly and just as definitively. In the parking lot a half-hour ago, and five years before, he knew. He'd been saying it to himself for five years—1,825 days, 43,800 hours, 2,628,000 minutes and counting. Jude might not know much anymore: why it happened, why they were left to pick up the pieces, what other nightmares lurked just out of sight, or how to fight them. But he knew this.

"It was a disaster," Eva conceded with a tired shake of her head. "That night? It was the biggest, baddest structure fire I've ever seen, I could tell that from the air. The kind of thing that you don't get out of alive without a miracle. And everybody's luck runs out sometime." She smiled, but it looked more like a pained grimace. "We lost a good man—a good friend. Jasper lost a fiance. But Felix went in with his eyes open, he knew the risks and so did Jasper. We all did. It was a known hazard. Not some demon."

"You weren't there, Eva!" He raised his voice without thinking about it, not a shout, more a plea. He couldn't sit still another second. He got to his feet and started to pace, pizza and plates forgotten. "You were a mile away in a helicopter. You didn't see it! How fast this thing moved, how sharp those teeth were, the claws, the way it just ripped right through—"

"I saw enough," she said resolutely, clearly refusing to rise to his desperate level. "The explosion. What was left, the charred... none of that came from a monster. But there were no claw marks, no bites."

"Because the burns covered everything up!" Jude tried to control his rising panic and mostly succeeded. His heart started to pound, but he'd cut and run once tonight already. Not again. "And you had to have heard it over the radio. We were all screaming loud enough."

"Are we really doing this, Jude?" Slowly, Eva rose to her feet too but didn't take a step, instead fixing him with a steady stare and holding her ground. "You really want to go back there?"

"Pretty sure we're already there," he said, forcing himself to stop moving and face her across the sofa back, which he gripped with both hands. Jude tried to keep the years of loss, terror, and frustration out of his voice, but his eyes narrowed and a hot flush spread across his pale cheeks. Some things you could only keep inside so long before they bubbled over, or burst out like a monster's full-moon howl. "Been there for five years."

"Un-be-*liev*-able," Eva said with a completely mirthless laugh, shaking her head at him and staring as if she'd never seen him before in her life. "You honestly think you're the only one who—God, Jude, we all went through hell! Put yourself in Jasper's place, for five minutes. Or mine! Trying to hold all of us together so we can have some kind of functional life."

"I know," he said, trying desperately to regain some equilibrium, but with every second his grip on the situation faltered, and he felt their connection slipping through his fingers. He gripped the sofa back more tightly, suddenly feeling like he might fall if he let go. "But I can't just bury it. I wish I could. But I can't ignore what happened—"

"*It didn't just happen to you!*" she burst out, shocking him into silence. "It happened to all of us! So how the hell do we move on after that? I don't know! But I'm still trying! Because if we don't, it'll eat us alive."

"Maybe you can move on, but I can't," he said, words blunt and voice hard. Too tired to soften a single one. Too tired to be anything but honest. "We lost Felix. I lost my leg. And my heart stopped. Everything stopped. Time stopped. It hasn't really started up again ever since."

"I know," Eva said, the fire in her voice dying down until she sounded as exhausted as he was, just as unable to escape the bone-deep fatigue and inescapable weight, the anchor that pulled them inexorably back to one devastating night under a full moon.

"I was gone for sixty seconds," he said, and now it was his turn to let out a laugh with no humor in it at all. "I come back and everything's different. Everything's gone. Felix is gone, and so are we. Who we used to be, our whole life. I'm here now, but I'm still gone. And now I can't stop seeing fangs."

Eva didn't answer. For a while, neither of them said a word.

"I know how it sounds," Jude said at last, and now the plea came through loud and clear. To be believed, to be supported, to have someone tell him to take a break, they'd handle it, it wasn't his problem. Say he didn't have to face every night alone ever again. "But I never told anything but the truth."

"I'm sorry I couldn't back you up," she returned softly, and truly sounded like it. "But I was telling the truth too."

"There are monsters out there. There really are."

"I know there are." She looked into his haunted eyes and, in hers, he saw five years' worth of fatigue and resolve, sleepless nights and isolated days. It felt like looking in a mirror. "But why do you have to be the one to fight them? Why do you have to carry the world on your shoulders?"

"I…" Jude couldn't continue. He could barely breathe.

The parking lot. Two terrifying creatures baring their teeth, eyes that blazed into his soul like high-beam headlights. He shivered, muscles twitching in an echo of the way he'd frozen, paralyzed as they laughed, then whispered, then flew away. Why did he have to be the one to face them? He couldn't remember the answer.

"We don't need to lose anything else," Eva said, and her voice was gentle now. Not an imperative, not a pragmatic declaration. Almost a plea of her own. "Or anyone. I don't want you to end up like…"

"Like Felix," he whispered, heart sinking. He leaned heavily against the sofa back. His knees felt weak. Both of them. His left leg burned in a phantom-limb fire.

"Like Jasper." Eva was more hugging herself than folding her arms now. She wasn't looking at Jude anymore, and he could barely make out her words.

"I'd say he's doing better than me," Jude offered with a shrug, though the casualness was deceptive. He'd heard the truth in her voice, but he didn't want to. "Jasper doesn't go looking for monsters in the dead of night. Or reach for the holy water when someone knocks on his door."

"No, he…" Eva stopped, and gave a sad shake of her head, shoulders sagging. "He doesn't. In a way, I almost wish he did. At least then I'd know how to reach him."

"They're out there," Jude said, but it sounded weak even to his own ears. A last, fragile defense that he didn't know was worth maintaining anymore. "I don't know how to explain it to you, but they are."

"I know there are monsters out there, Jude." The shake in Eva's voice couldn't just be his imagination. "But they're human. I'm not saying forget everything, I'm not saying don't feel it, I'm just…God, we've earned a break. You've earned a night safe at home watching TV, eating pizza. I've earned a life that makes sense. We deserve that."

"I know," he murmured.

"Jude." Her voice was soft. He heard her take a step, then felt her hands on his shoulders. "It's you, me and Jasper. We're all that's left. We're all we have left, each other. That's all. If something happens to you, how long do you think he'll—"

"I know," he said as he looked up, voice a little stronger. Eva didn't want to hear a lot of things. Jude didn't want to hear however she was going to finish that last sentence. "I'm sorry."

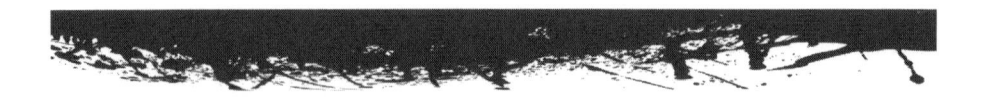

"I just don't want to be the last one." He felt the pressure increase on his shoulders just a little. She wasn't squeezing so much as leaning on him, like he'd done with the sofa. Like him, it felt like without the support, she might fall. "I'm tired. Aren't you tired?"

Jude thought about going one night without jumping at a shadow. He thought about sleep.

"All right," he said at last. "No more late nights. No more chasing monsters. No more…" He thought about the way his blood turned to ice in his veins, and his heart clenched in his chest at the sight of fangs gleaming sharp and deadly in a streetlight, bright as the full moon. "No more vampires."

"Thank you," she said, letting her breath out in a rush, and squeezing his shoulders. "That's all I needed to hear. Now eat."

"I already had a slice," he said, but it wasn't an actual argument. Her faint smile told him they were back on safe, familiar ground.

"Get another one. You can go back to forgetting food exists as soon as I leave, but as long as I'm here, you're gonna eat."

"I'll try to remember," he said, grabbing a second slice and pouring some more red sauce. This time he didn't keep it contained to a small pool in the corner. It was a lot better when it covered the entire cheesy triangle.

"Write yourself a damn sticky note, set an alarm. Just take care of yourself." She didn't bother to hide her fondness as she watched him take another bite, eyes widening as the rich, mildly spicy sauce woke his neglected taste buds up after a long hibernation. "Oh, you like that? Good, I've got about a hundred bottles in my kitchen. You can have it all."

"What is it?" Jude asked, curious in spite of himself. He couldn't remember the last time he'd actually been interested in something that wasn't undead and fanged. Sometimes it was nice to be reminded there was more to life.

"Mags says it's supposed to be like, fancy experimental gourmet stuff,"

Eva said with a faint eye-roll that jogged Jude's memory. Magnolia was every bit as tough and outspoken as her big sister, but where Eva had dedicated her life to fighting fires, Magnolia and her husband Dorian kept their burns controlled and productive—in their restaurant's open-flame kitchen. "One of Dorian's old family recipes, all traditional from the Old Country. I'm supposed to be selling it, but I can't give the stuff away."

"Why?" Jude frowned, taking another big bite. "It's good."

"Oh I know! I love it too, especially this kind, I think that's the—" Eva shut her mouth, eyes growing wide.

"What?" Jude shot her a look, not missing her hesitation, or letting the moment of weirdness pass. She certainly never did when their positions were reversed. "It's what?"

"Nothing. Forget I said anything." Eva said, looking down to nervously eye the remains of her own sauce. She was a terrible liar. So was Jude, but he liked to think he was at least a little smoother than her. Most people were.

"What's going on, Eva?" Jude frowned, picking up the bottle and giving it a suspicious once-over. "What's in this stuff?"

"Oh... nothing!" Her voice rose in pitch, and she let out a short laugh. "It's just, you know, fancy-pants hipster bullshit, all pretentious, artisan, way too expensive—"

"Eva."

"Blood." She leaned heavily back against the counter, pressing the heels of her hands against her eyes. "They have a lot of different recipes, and I think that's the blood one. Some creepy Transylvanian—no, actually, I think this one's Italian—except instead of blood pudding or sausage or whatever, they decided 'okay, we'll make a steak sauce and sell it, everyone will barbecue with blood, not just on Halloween but every day, this is a great idea, *Keep Portland Weird!*'" When she was done, she sounded a little out of breath.

"Huh." Jude hesitated, dipping his pinkie fingertip into the sauce and studying it. After a second he stuck it in his mouth, considering. Yes, it still tasted delicious, even knowing what was in it. Even knowing his history with things that drank blood. He should have found it repulsive, but instead, something about enjoying it himself seemed... triumphant. The corners of his mouth turned up into a smile, and he nodded as he held up the red bottle. "Still good. I'm keeping it."

"Okay," she said, considerably more calmly. "That's one bottle down. Ninety-nine on the wall to go."

"What about your cousin, um, Layla?" He frowned, trying to remember several years back, before their lives had been shaken up and distorted beyond recognition by smoke, fire and blood. "You took me to a dinner she gave once? There was a ton of great food, lots of people. You could probably give a bunch to them."

Eva gave him a long-suffering look. "My extended family's Muslim, you doorknob. That was an after-Ramadan feast."

"Huh?"

"I can't give them that. Against their religion? They don't eat gross things like blood sauce—or anything made with blood. Unlike some people, who think wine literally... you know, that long trans-word I can't pronounce. Not 'transgender,'" she said with a smile. "You walked me through all that."

"Transubstantiation," Jude sighed, the syllables rolling automatically right off his tongue. They carried old-but-unfaded memories of school uniforms, black-robed nuns leading morning prayers, sweaty kids packed close in together for special occasion services, jokes about whether saints ever stepped in during finals.

"That's the one. Wine literally turning into the holy body and blood? I don't get Catholics. No offense."

"I'm... a lapsed Catholic." He shook his head, bringing himself back to the present. Some memories weren't overtly traumatic, at least in the horror-and-death way, but he still didn't like to spend too much time in them. "Very lapsed. I don't get us either."

Eva gave him another, more thoughtful look. "Jude, when you changed your name, you picked a saint. Even an aimless, lapsed Baptist like me knows that."

"Patron Saint of Lost Causes," he said with an appreciative nod. "It was very meaningful at the time." A grimace crossed his face, as if he'd just tasted or smelled something vastly unpleasant. "Then the goddamn Beatles came along."

Eva laughed. "*Then* they came along? Think you're about fifty years too late." She shook her head and headed toward the door. "Finish that pizza. And the sauce. Then I can shove another bottle off on you."

"Aren't you supposed to be selling these?" he called after her, then followed, quickly starting to undo his seven locks. "Do I owe you anything?"

"Pay me back by staying home at night and doing your job in the daytime," she said, leaning against the wall as he finished the last lock and opened the door. "Honestly, I just appreciate you taking the stuff off my hands. Can't wait to have some counter space again."

When Eva left, the apartment was very quiet, and Jude was alone with his thoughts. He had even more tonight than usual. But for once, they weren't entirely about deep shadows and sharp fangs.

✵ XII THE HANGED MAN ✵

ACT TWO:
Of Lost Causes

SOMETIMES, JUDE was actually glad the mall was so overstimulating. Headache-inducing or not, its bright lights and crowd chatter drummed any thoughts of fanged horrors out of his head—here, they seemed ridiculous. This was the real world, and nothing he was scared of belonged. The shadows didn't run miles deep. Nightmares and half-buried memories faded in the face of neon lights and sale signs. Everything seemed familiar, friendly, and reasonable in the sun.

But the main promenade wasn't his ultimate destination. He'd get out on the floor soon. He'd meant it when he told Eva he'd actually do his job, but one last loose end remained. Or a last chance. The light of day made him brave enough to take it. He turned into a small corner shop, bearing a sign reading Jasper's Rare Finds: Vintage Books and Records in curling, elegant lettering.

Jude blinked a few times as he crossed the threshold. It was always darker in Jasper's store than in the brightly lit mall, and more cramped. Every bit of shelf and floor space was crammed with books, records and mysterious-looking items. Crystal balls that had to be fake. A large, rune-covered skull that Jude certainly hoped was. It all made for an impressively arcane atmosphere, like every book or antique might be hiding something and, if they weren't, anyone who frequented this place probably was.

Jude was almost certain this place was a front for something else, dealing in illicit materials not found on its visible shelves—what, he didn't care to hazard a guess. Ordinarily lawful in the extreme, Jude made one glaring exception. As long as Jasper wasn't hurting anyone else, or himself, he deserved whatever coping mechanism worked, however shady. The only warning signs, so far, were Jasper's evasive answers about his job's specifics and the occasional unsavory or enigmatic person hanging around his store.

Jude had passed one on the way over. A few small tables stood near the store's entrance, overflow from the nearby coffee shop. The one nearest to the doorway was occupied by a pale woman all in black, complete with a floppy-brimmed hat and oversized sunglasses, sitting alone and shuffling a deck of cards. Every time he'd come here, actually, she seemed to be there with her cards and tall coffee. Jude never asked, but he had to wonder if Jasper actually paid her to sit there and add to the mysterious ambiance. Much stranger things had happened. At one point her presence had made Jude decidedly nervous—pale strangers tended to do that—but after the first few times, he'd concluded she was probably just an older example of the mall goths who frequented The Abyss. Jude had never been inside; the colorful hair and loud music repelled him, and at least none of the clientele had yet shown fangs.

"Jasper? Are you even in here?" There was barely room to pick his way through the labyrinthine shelves and piles of books sitting on the floor. Jasper would call it 'cozy' or 'atmospheric.' Jude called it a mess.

"Mmm," came the noncommittal response. Jasper stood behind the counter, round shoulders hunched as he pored over yet another thick, leather-bound book. He hadn't looked up when Jude entered, and didn't now.

He was heavyset and not much older than Jude's 25, but he'd clearly made an effort to look otherwise. His face was hidden by the brim of a large black top hat and, under it, his thick dark hair was disheveled. Deceptively so, Jude knew just how long it took to tease it into the perfect shape and frizz level.

"I need to talk to you," Jude said, finally emerging from the shop's maze.

Every book he could see was old, decades or maybe centuries, but well-preserved. Nothing was overtly ominous, but the dim light and arcane aesthetics put him in a certain state of mind, one he never liked to linger in. He couldn't wait to see fluorescent lights.

"Of course. Anything." Today's costume didn't look like Wednesday's usual, now that he could see it properly. Wednesday usually involved plaid, but this one instead gave the impression of a circus ringleader or cabaret Master of Ceremonies. A bright red silk scarf contrasted with his black and white tuxedo and tails, and there seemed to be a very fine layer of glitter over all of him, and a bit on the nearby countertop. But what Jude could see of the book on the counter was clean and glitter-free. It looked very old and the writing on its weathered, parchment-like pages was small and in a language he didn't recognize. Apparently Jasper did, because he smiled, as if he'd just read something funny. He still didn't look up.

"It's about..." Jude lowered his voice and tried to make the near-whisper as intense as possible. Sometimes drama worked when not much else did. "...*Them.*"

Jasper casually turned a page. "Anything but that."

"It's important," Jude said at a regular volume and his normal, if slightly annoyed, voice.

"So is deciphering Ms. Verazza's latest enigma." Now Jasper looked up, and his entire ensemble came together. His heavy eyeliner came down into points halfway down a theatrically pale face and black-polished nails gleamed in the low, faux-candlelight as he folded his hands and rested his elbows on the front desk. Gothic ringleader, Jude thought, a little appreciatively despite himself. With some creepy harlequin. "That woman is taunting me, I can just feel it."

"If she wrote that," Jude said, nodding down to the yellowed pages and dense scrawls, "she has to be taunting you from beyond the grave. How old is that thing?"

"At least a-hundred-and-fifty years," Jasper said, casting the book a baleful glance as if it were indeed smugly mocking him. "And, for the past week, it's been quite the headache. You wouldn't happen to have heard of a 'burned angel,' have you? Who 'sleeps in the circle of stones?'"

"Is that some kind of riddle?" Jude frowned, wary of being pulled into some game for which he really wasn't in the mood. He'd always gotten the feeling Jasper's side businesses involved more than old books. Magic, if he was to be believed. Jude wasn't sure how much he did believe. His brain rebelled at the existence of vampires, much less anything else. He'd never really inquired about specifics and he'd never seen Jasper do anything more ethereal than morph his hair and makeup from one persona to another. He was also a firm believer in using whatever coping mechanism worked, no matter how unorthodox.

"You tell me." Jasper shot Jude a quick grin, raising his eyebrows in a very expectant way. Clearly he *was* in the mood for games. Color Jude unsurprised.

"I don't know." Jude shook his head, glancing back out toward the wide open mall and its tempting, brightly lit spaces and complete absence of non-sequiturs. Maybe coming in here had been a mistake.

"Are you all right?" The slightly provocative smile slipped off Jasper's face and his pale blue eyes turned searching instead of playful. "You look like you haven't slept in days."

"More like nights," Jude admitted, with some regret and more fatigue. "A few nights."

"Bad dreams?" Coming from anyone else, the question would have seemed invasive, or teasing. But despite the glint he'd had in his eyes a moment ago, Jasper seemed nothing but sincere and concerned. More than that, he sounded like he had experience. Both of these impressions, Jude knew, were accurate.

"Old ones." Jude ran a hand through his hair and rubbed the back of his sore neck. He hadn't gotten much sleep since Eva left last night, unable to stop replaying everything she'd said, and everything he'd seen in the parking lot earlier. "The kind that don't go away when I wake up."

"Well, if there's any way I can help," Jasper offered, serious and sympathetic. "I'll do it in a heartbeat, you know that."

"You could back me up." Jude leaned forward in an uncharacteristically conspiratorial way, resting his own elbows on the counter. He'd seen Jasper utilize space and nonverbal communication to emphasize his points enough times to give it a try himself, no matter how silly it felt. "I'm done, I really am, but Eva still thinks I imagined the whole thing, and I just don't want it to end like that. And you can tell her I'm not making it up, and I'm not just seeing things. I'm not that far gone yet."

"Oh." Jasper immediately looked back down at his book, seeming to find something in its inscrutable text deeply intriguing. "No, I'm sorry, I don't think that would be a good idea."

"Why not?" Jude asked, a little more loudly than he'd intended, and straightened up, frustration shaking his focus.

"Many reasons," Jasper said, with a firmness clearly meant to discourage argument, which might have worked on anyone who wasn't Jude. "None of which would do any good to drag back up to the surface."

"This is important," Jude insisted, intent on finding at least one ally. Common sense and good advice told him to give it all up without question—but he couldn't stand the thought of his best friends thinking he was misguided at best and completely out of touch with reality at worst. Especially when he'd seen firsthand evidence to the contrary. "I told Eva I wasn't doing this anymore—"

"Oh, good for you!"

"I said I *would* stop." Jasper chuckled at this, and Jude had the sudden urge to grab the top hat off his head. Didn't know what he'd do with it, but it would get his attention. "And I will. Soon."

"You lied to Eva?" Now Jasper peered up from underneath his hat, interest seeming piqued.

"No, I didn't lie," Jude said slowly, trying to sound as reasonable and grounded in reality as possible. Being in this particular shop, and talking with its owner, always made that difficult. "She told me to let the past go and focus on the present, and she's right, and I will. Very soon."

"You lied to Eva," Jasper concluded, nose back in the book. "Your funeral."

"I saw them," Jude lowered his voice again to an intense whisper. "Last night. In the parking lot."

"You saw something strange in the parking lot?" Jasper said with a dry laugh, not looking up. "Alert the media."

"It was them!" Jude insisted. "The two girls? I've been catching more and more glimpses lately, and last night I got closer than I ever have—"

"Oh, God love you, Jude," Jasper said with a sigh and a slow shake of his head. "You're a lost cause."

"It's the truth and you know it. All of it," Jude said softly, resisting the urge to glance over his shoulder. They were the only ones in here, standing close enough to speak in whispers, but he still felt exposed and vulnerable whenever he said certain things out loud. "You were there. You saw everything I did. Eva didn't, but I know you did."

"That's certainly true," Jasper said briskly. His eyes scanned the page, but Jude had the distinct impression that he wasn't reading a word anymore. "I saw a lot of things. Felt them. Heard, smelled, tasted even, it was a five-sense experience. And that's how I developed a *sixth* sense for things that are better left alone."

"So you're giving up?" Jude asked, equal parts disappointed and incredulous.

"Yes!" Jasper raised his voice beyond low conversational tones for the first time and his bright blue eyes flashed in a glare as he lifted his head. Jude wasn't often on the receiving end of one of those. He sometimes forgot exactly how much intensity Jasper could command, this was a reminder. "And I've said it before, you would too if you had half the sense Eva thinks you do."

"Well, that's not much."

"My point exactly."

Jude glanced around at the store full of old books, crystals, skulls, and objects he couldn't even identify, and resisted comment. "Don't you want to find the things that attacked us that night?"

"*Thing.*" Jasper's sharp eyes narrowed, a sudden undercurrent of cold anger in his voice. All at once, his dark ringleader costume and harlequinesque makeup seemed a lot more menacing. There were a lot of creatures Jude had no desire to run into in a dark alley and, for the first time, he got the feeling that Jasper was not only prepared to meet them, but would have a better chance of surviving than he did. "There was only one."

"I know. The one that killed Felix. Isn't that—"

"Don't talk about him like that, please." Jasper closed the book with a soft *thud*. His voice dropped, and there was no sharp edge to his words, but Jude knew better than to push him. Jude had seen the way Eva froze, hearing that name. He probably did the same whenever someone mentioned it. Jasper didn't freeze, really, but he did push himself back from the counter that Jude felt much more tangibly as a barrier between them, everything about his face and voice seeming to close off and invite no pursuit. "Let's not use his memory to win arguments."

"I'm sorry," Jude said, wishing for not the first time that life came with a rewind button instead of existential dread and fanged menaces. Going back a few seconds, or a few years, both ideas were tantalizing. "I didn't—I'm sorry."

"No, I am." Jasper's sequin-dusted shoulders sagged and every bit of energy their quick back-and-forth had built up seemed to seep out of the room as he sighed, leaving Jude cold. He took off his hat and started to rub at his temples and tightly-shut eyes. "That was uncalled-for. You weren't trying to... you cared about him too. You understand."

Jasper put his warm hand briefly on Jude's arm and squeezed, before taking a few steps away and sinking his heavy frame down into a rarely-occupied reading chair half-hidden by the counter. Jude always had suspected it wasn't actually for customers. Jasper shut his eyes and rested his forehead in his hands, hat laying forgotten on the counter.

"Another migraine?" Jude asked, lowering his voice as he had before, but this time it wasn't to be dramatic.

"Or something like it..." Jasper didn't look up, also as before, but not to play a game. "Regular stuff isn't working. Might have to break out something stronger. At least it's legal now."

"Your pain's getting worse?" Jude's voice sharpened involuntarily, and he felt a pang of adrenaline. Worry felt like nausea, but colder.

"Not getting any better, that's for sure." He let out a long sigh, seeming to deflate. He murmured something. Maybe Jude wasn't supposed to hear but he caught the tail end anyway, "only thing that used to help..."

"What used to help?" Jude asked quickly, still feeling energized and propelled into action despite having nothing useful to actually do.

A slight pause. When the answer came, it was mumbled and flat. "Felix's hands."

Jude hesitated, holding very still. "I'm not meaning to pry—"

"By all means, pry away," Jasper actually laughed, but it wasn't a happy sound. "It'll distract me."

"I thought your head started hurting after... that night," Jude said, with the fervent hope he wasn't about to hear something that would make their strained days and desolate nights even worse. "Is it something else now?"

"I've always had migraines," Jasper said, massaging his temples. "But yes, they did get much worse five years ago. Blunt force trauma will do that."

"I'm sorry," Jude said, because he couldn't think of anything else. That was a regular problem.

"Felix helped with all of it, before." Jasper said, continuing to rub at his head in what seemed to be a poor substitute. "His hands were amazing—I guess you don't get to be a medic unless you have them. They always knew exactly where it hurt, and how to take the pain away. And so gentle. Like the rest of him. Magical hands, always where they were needed most." In the brief pause that followed, he glanced up, and Jude caught the faintest ghost of familiar amusement in his eye. "Yes, I'm still talking about headaches."

"Of course," Jude said, only a little deadpan.

"But now that you mention it..." The sharp, slightly mischievous ringleader smile crept back onto Jasper's face, like he was about to welcome a captive audience to the greatest show in the underworld. "His hands were good for lots of things besides migraines. My favorite was—"

"All right," Jude held up his own hands, but he was far from actually bothered, instead, deeply relieved to find himself back on solid ground. Jude had a very low tolerance for teasing under most circumstances, but when Jasper did it, the world made a little more sense. "I have a pretty good imagination."

"As if you'd have to imagine!" Jasper actually laughed, and this one sounded much more genuine than his previous sardonic chuckles. "You knew we'd end up together before I did. And you're blushing. You are!"

"I am not!" Jude protested, even as his hand flew up to his cheek to check. It was warm, which he knew it would be. Jasper had gotten under his skin again, this time without even trying. But the weariness and pain were gone from his face, and it even seemed like his head didn't hurt quite as badly. An even trade.

"You were right, though, we did belong together. Sometimes you have to take a leap of faith. And adrenaline is an addictive substance."

"Addictive." Jude couldn't help but smile. "Really."

"The only thing better than jumping out of a helicopter, running into a burning building, or asking someone to marry you is live theatre." He adjusted his red silk scarf and sequined collar. "Or so I've heard."

They both fell silent, comfortably so. Jude rarely felt the need to fill up quiet rooms with meaningless words, and never with Jasper or Eva. With them, he wouldn't have cared if it stretched on all day. He knew exactly how rare and wonderful that was, to have two people in his life he could say that about. He'd once had three, but he still counted himself lucky.

"I would have loved to be your best man," he said at last. It was hard to get the words out, but not because they weren't true. Quite the opposite. The truer and more important something was, the harder verbalizing it seemed to be. "If things had gone differently. I wish they'd gone differently."

"Me too," Jasper answered mildly. His tone was light and noncommittal, revealing nothing. He didn't have to. It hurt anyway.

"Just the fact that you asked me..." Jude continued, suddenly finding words pale, clumsy things, not at all what he needed to express the never-ending gratitude and deep warmth he carried with him through the bleakest of nights. "Best man. Man, specifically—you don't know how much that means. I don't think you can."

"We had some idea," Jasper said, an answering fondness in his voice. "But you're right, some things no one can really understand unless they live it. I'm glad we could give that to you."

"You were the first I told. Before Eva, even."

Jasper looked up now, eyes clearing and wide with what looked like slight surprise and deeper emotion. "Even her? I didn't know that."

"You were the first to call me by my name." Jude nodded, swallowing past the thickening feeling in his throat. All this time, and he'd never told Jasper any of this. Maybe he should have, years ago. They both knew firsthand the importance of making sure loved ones knew exactly how important they were, while the chance remained. "You called me a man for the first time in my life."

"Well," Jasper said, slowly rising to his feet and replacing his hand on Jude's arm. This time he didn't move away. "We always did think you were the best."

It took Jude a moment to clear his eyes and even longer to speak. "There's really nothing I can do, is there?"

"Just listening helps." Jasper's face was soft under the dark, sharp-lined makeup. "Talking about him helps. I don't do it enough." His eyes narrowed again then, tone turning a little bitter. "Or maybe I do it too much, I don't really know anymore."

"I don't know if there is a too much." Jude tried to maintain the connection they'd enjoyed for these few minutes, a deep understanding that made him like feel part of the world again instead of isolated from it. He knew it was good for Jasper too, but he could feel the distance between them growing, just like Eva last night. There was only so much either of them could handle before the pain got too close, even in memories. "Not when you lose someone like that. I hope you find some peace, Jasper."

Jasper replaced his hat and shot Jude a smile that came nowhere near reaching his eyes. "After five years, I'm lucky if I can find my way home."

🔥

The walk home was short and blissfully silent. Jude barely saw anything, eyes out of focus and feet carrying him back to Sunset Towers—his usual, vampire free route—the way he did most things, by muscle memory. He'd already hit the lights, made it into the kitchen, and opened the fridge when he heard it. A soft noise, half-knocking, half-scratching, like someone fumbling with the doorknob with their hands full.

"Eva?" He called, poking his head back out of the kitchen. His living room was actually feeling warm and almost homey, a far cry from the tense atmosphere from the night before. It was amazing what a good conversation with a trusted friend could do. Even if he was on his own when it came to vampires—which he was done chasing, he reminded himself, so this was quickly becoming a moot point—and even if Jasper was clearly still in a much worse place than he'd like to admit, Jude couldn't help but feel better about everything. He'd made the right decision, and he wasn't alone, not really. Maybe this was how healing started.

"Come on in, enjoy some delicious blood sauce," he laughed a little at himself, hand on the doorknob. "How much of that stuff did you say you had? 99 bottles? Was that a joke, or—"

CRASH.

Shards of glass and wood showered the living room as something exploded through the nearby window. Jude barely caught a glimpse of a shadowy form topped with a flash of pink as he dove behind the couch, heart in his mouth as he tried to gauge the distance between himself and his next course of action.

Back in the kitchen, grab the holy water? Too far, by precious seconds. Bedroom? Required leaving his cover. He couldn't even see well enough to make a choice that didn't end in death—whatever it was had knocked over a lamp and shattered the bulb in a shower of sparks, halving the light and casting strange, flickering shadows up across the walls and ceiling.

Every option opened himself to attack from whoever—or whatever—had just slammed into his living room like an asteroid. Paralyzed by indecision and fighting panic, Jude held perfectly still and did nothing at all.

A few seconds went by, silence broken only by his own shallow breathing. Then:

"*Ow.*"

Jude didn't recognize the voice. And couldn't tell from the single word where the intruder was. He waited a little longer, but nothing met his ears but more silence, and the whistling of a cold night wind through his now-broken window. Finally, very slowly, he peered out from behind the couch.

He had one chair that matched the old sofa, and now it was tipped over along with the lamp, lying on its back on the floor. In it, a young man sprawled, upside-down and legs in the air, looking like he'd just stepped out of a punk rock concert, or maybe off the stage. His jeans were torn, his hair was bright pink, and his ears were full of piercings—large, unusually pointed ears. His only concession to the cold outside was a scarf pulled tight around his neck, black, covered in tiny red skulls, and with the tags still hanging from it. New at best, stolen at worst. The whole ensemble would have been at home at some loud, chaotically anarchist gathering Jude would have wanted to leave immediately. But none of that actually added up to intimidation, at least not while he was down on the floor. If this was a burglar, he was about the most ineffective one Jude had ever seen.

And he made no effort to move, folding his hands across his soft, round belly and staring up at the ceiling. Didn't even seem hurt or distressed, more like he was getting his bearings and taking a quick break. For the few seconds it took both of them to adjust, he stayed right where he'd landed.

When Jude managed to speak, his own voice was surprisingly calm, considering. "What the fuck?"

The uninvited guest stared up at him, a matching expression of confusion on his upside-down face. "You're the one who invited me in."

"I did not," Jude said automatically.

"Yes you did, I heard you, just now, you said 'let yourself in.' So I did."

"I wasn't talking to you!"

The pink-haired intruder shrugged, or did the closest movement possible while lying on his back. "Sorry. My bad."

"Your bad..." Jude repeated, raising his eyebrows in bewilderment, suddenly aware of how absurd all this was. He was arguing with a young punk—exactly the kind of delinquent who made Jude's reluctant job harder every day, the kind who threw things at Eva, the kind that still hadn't righted himself or gotten up off the floor. "This is my apartment. And that *was* my window."

"Yeah..." Now he slowly sat up, brushing small bits of glass off his shoulders and back. He seemed only slightly sore rather than actually hurt by his sudden and exciting entrance. He'd come through in a lot better shape than Jude's window, at least. "Sorry about that. Windows just kind of sneak up, you know?"

"No," Jude shook his head, actually impressed at exactly how calm he was staying. "I don't. I don't know anything. Like what you're doing here... Pixie."

"Hey, you remember!" Jude's upstairs neighbor had always been distinctive. The bright hair and shiny piercings, his small, chubby build made of soft curves and few sharp angles. The way his nose wrinkled up a little when he smiled (infuriatingly, that was the exact look he'd had right before Jude had told him to turn his music down, the *exact one)*. The big, pointed ears with their rows of studs and hoops, which gave a little twitch, as if he knew Jude was looking at them specifically.

"You're kind of hard to forget. I thought you were missing," Jude said, relieved despite his frustration and everything else about this moment. This was unmistakably Pixie, from the pink hair to the unlikely name. Still, something he couldn't quite place was bothering him. Besides his window, lamp, and glass-covered floor.

"How can I be missing if I'm right here?" Pixie seemed to find the idea amusing. Jude didn't, eyes narrowing as he peered closer, trying to get a better look in the too-low light.

"Something's different about you." Jude was sure of that, but still couldn't say why. It wasn't his hair, although that had changed since Jude had seen him. Last time they'd clashed it had been an electric blue, appropriately sticking straight up as if he'd stuck his toe in a wall socket. It wasn't even the scarf or the T-shirt Jude had never seen before, ripped in a way that might have been intentional, reading *'Chaos Chainsaw.'* Was that a band? A singer? A too-strong drink? So much baffled him tonight.

"Well, you look the same as ever," Pixie said, still sounding upbeat and eager to make a good first impression. He could start by repairing the window. "Jude, right?"

"That's right," he said, studying his impromptu nighttime visitor and resisting the urge to show him out the way he'd come in.

"*Hey, Ju*—uh," Pixie stopped as Jude's face hardened into an immediate glare. He'd put up with a lot tonight and that would have just been the last straw. If even Eva and Jasper weren't allowed to tease him like that—not that they would on purpose, they knew how he felt about it—this guy absolutely wasn't. A sheepish grin spread across Pixie's face, and he pointed up with two black-nailed fingers. "Dude. Hey, dude, how's it going?"

"It's quieter. Haven't had to make a noise complaint in the past month."

"You never did appreciate my music," the younger man said primly, getting up off the floor. He talked as if he had some kind of high ground despite being surrounded by broken glass. Which he'd shattered.

"No, I don't. And I asked you very politely—"

"Pff, banging on your ceiling is polite? You almost punched a hole in my floor!"

"I had to get your attention somehow, since apparently asking five or six times wasn't good enough!"

"Everybody's a music critic!"

"That was not music." Jude folded his arms while Pixie clapped a hand to his chest and gasped as if mortally offended. "I don't know what that was, but it wasn't music, it wasn't anything I've ever—"

"Excuse me!" Pixie's large ears twitched again as he took a step closer, looking up at a sharp angle at the taller Jude, who stared unflinchingly right back down. "I don't criticize your taste in whatever it is *you* like!"

"No, you just burst into my apartment at night, almost give me a heart attack, and shatter my window! You still haven't told me what you *want*."

"Want?" Pixie let out a giggle that sounded distinctly nervous. "Can't a guy just, uh, wanna come see a fr—not a friend, just another guy, a familiar—"

"Familiar is right," Jude squinted again, leaning down closer. Pixie held very still, not even blinking, as if he were even holding his breath. "But there's still something different about you. I just can't put my finger on it."

"Uh, I don't know what you mean." Pixie started to bounce quickly on the balls of his feet, as if holding still for just those few seconds had taken all the self-control he had. "Oh—it's probably the hair. Or the earrings! I got a few new studs."

"No, I'm used to all of those..." Jude waved vaguely at the alternative accessories, and didn't stop studying Pixie's face. Maybe it was just the low light (the broken one Jude would make him pay for later along with the window), but the young man's skin looked almost ashen grey.

"Um, so, what'd I miss while I was gone?" Pixie asked brightly, clearly trying to change the subject. "Anything exciting happen around here?"

"No," Jude answered after a moment's hesitation. He was unwilling to let his vague but undeniable suspicion go, but something Pixie said had only deepened it. "Wait. 'While you were gone?' Where have you been?"

"Uh, around," Pixie deflected and looked away, back out the window, and now Jude could swear his ears drooped just a little. He reached up to nervously adjust his scarf. "Um, did anyone ask about me? Come looking?"

"Some police came by," Jude spoke slowly, watching for any telling reaction. He had the definite impression Pixie was making just as concerted an effort to control himself, and Jude caught the widening of his eyes and the small catch of his breath. "My friend Eva said you'd gone missing. They must have been here to check it out. Have you been back to your apartment at all?"

"Uh, yeah, sure." Pixie swallowed, eyes flicking again to the broken window. Jude knew that look well. Pixie was doing what he'd done just a moment ago. Gauging distance, time, ease of making a fast escape. "Hey, you don't happen to remember what these cops look like, do you?"

"What are you asking me?" Jude gave him a hard look, less annoyed and more suspicious with every passing moment. "Pixie, are you in some kind of trouble?"

"Ha, no!" He laughed just a little too loudly. Jude had seen his share of terrible liars (and been one) long enough to recognize when someone was floundering. "What? No, come on, what would I even—no!"

"Listen," Jude dropped his voice, then his folded arms. "I work mall security, but that's not why I'm asking. I'm not with the police and I don't talk to them either."

"Really?" Pixie asked, voice rising in pitch as he took a step away from Jude and toward the window. "'Cause it's kinda hard to tell the difference from where I'm standing."

"You came to me for a reason, didn't you? I can't help you if you don't—"

"I said no!" Pixie took another step back. As he did, his eyes flared, blue-green and chillingly familiar, iridescent like a cat's. His mouth, still open from his sharp cry, revealed sharp-pointed canines. Even as his pulse pounded loudly in his ears, Jude's blood ran cold.

He'd been right. There was something different about Pixie.

"*Shit.*"

They leaped away from one another. Jude flew toward his kitchen at last while Pixie stumbled backwards. Jude threw the emergency drawer open and, in a moment, the holy water was in his hand, stopper open. He acted on instinct, hurling the liquid toward the dark shape huddled in the corner and its still-glowing eyes.

A high-pitched, inhuman yowl split the silence. Jude scrambled backward, not looking to see the result, but feeling grimly satisfied as he shielded his head with his arms. But, although the vampire's bloodcurdling screeching continued, no talons raked down his back, no teeth sank into his skin. He wasn't being ripped to shreds. Something was wrong. Slowly, he lowered his hands and opened his eyes, turning around to face his opponent.

Pixie was right back where he'd started. On the floor. But he'd curled up in a ball, rolling around and covering his own head to escape imaginary blows. Instead of what Jude had thought was a bloodcurdling predatory shriek, he let out terrified squeals. Jude watched for a few seconds, dumbfounded, but nothing else happened. No lethal attacks, no mortal terror. Just increasing levels of secondhand embarrassment.

"Does it really hurt?" he asked, letting the hand holding the holy water drop and hang loose. Pixie didn't reply, not seeming to hear. The small... vampire, if the fangs and eyes were to be believed, continued to squirm in a tight, scared ball, yowls dissolving into sad whimpering noises. Jude pinched the bridge of his nose, a gesture that reminded him of Eva whenever she was particularly exasperated with him. One for which he now had a newfound empathy and respect. "Please stop."

Pixie didn't stop. His only response was to paw at one wet ear, rubbing every bit of holy water off his definitely-grey skin. Jude sighed and turned away, feeling safe enough to briefly leave the room. When he returned with a towel a moment later, the shivering vampire was still there, and hadn't uncurled. So he dropped the towel right on top of Pixie.

"Thank you," said the dripping lump under the towel.

"Mm-hmm." Jude stared, wondering all the while what in the hell he was doing and how to steer the situation back toward something he knew how to deal with. Fighting vampires was one thing. Having weird, awkward standoffs with them was another. When he spoke again, it was in a conversational tone even he found absurd. "So, it's true about holy water?"

"What?" Pixie emerged, hair standing up even straighter than usual from the vigorous toweling. "Oh. No, I guess not. It doesn't burn or anything. Which is good to know! I thought it would, honestly, learn something new every day. But you did scare the heck out of me. Also, I don't really like being wet."

"I scared *you?*" Jude stared some more, then shook his head with an aggravated snort. Enough. "Never mind—get out of here!"

"That's not very nice," Pixie grumbled, sounding hurt again.

"You're a vampire!" Jude exclaimed in an ever-more-familiar combination of frustration and confusion. "I should be staking you right now!"

"Do you actually have a stake?" Pixie asked, looking up sharply and looking legitimately worried for the first time.

Jude only hesitated for a second, hoping that he was, at least, not the worst liar in the room. "Maybe!"

"Well, thanks for not using it." Pixie seemed to relax a little, but continued to anxiously twist the towel in his hands. Something about his eyes, when they weren't flashing glare-bright, made Jude shut his mouth. His pupils were definitely more vertical than Jude was used to seeing but, aside from that, they looked almost human. "I don't even know if it'd work for sure either, but getting stabbed in the chest is never gonna sound fun. So, yeah, thanks for that."

"I'm... you're welcome." Jude folded his arms, somehow feeling like he'd just been out-maneuvered. The fact that he wasn't entirely sure if it was intentional didn't make it better. "You're still a vampire, in *my* house, which is about the worst place a vampire could ever be. You're dealing with an armed, dangerous, *prepared* vampire hunter." He held up the holy water and gave it an intimidating shake. Then realized the bottle was empty and quickly stopped.

"Okay, good." Pixie nodded, not actually looking as unimpressed as Jude had expected, but not that scared either. "That's actually why I'm here."

"You have a death wish?"

"I mean, I'm kind of already dead, so—"

"Just talk fast and get out of my apartment so I can fix my window!" Jude was shivering already, and it wasn't entirely from the adrenaline. Maybe cold didn't bother vampires, but it certainly bothered him, that and virtually everything else about this conversation.

Pixie did talk fast. "Okay! So the mall's infested, right? With a ton of pesky vampires who like to bug you, and kick me around, and basically act like bullies who own the place, right?" Pixie stopped and waited, looking like he expected Jude to agree immediately. When he didn't, he went on. "And they're really annoying, they scare people, they suck their blood, all kinds of, just, real bad things that vampires do, right? Except for me. I don't—I mean, they're out of control, someone should do something!"

"I intend to," Jude said levelly, and hopefully menacingly. Pixie apparently didn't know about his promise to Eva, to stop chasing vampires and start focusing on his actual job. And he didn't need to. Not yet, anyway, not while it gave Jude even a slight advantage. "I'm out there every night."

"Yeah, I know!" Pixie didn't sound nearly as scared of this as Jude had expected or intended. Again, frustrating.

"You do?" Jude narrowed his eyes, suspicion re-igniting. Vampiric nature aside, this one was up to something. "What do you know?"

"Um—I hear things." Pixie wiggled one large ear, apparently in a demonstration. When Jude didn't smile or otherwise acknowledge this, he quickly moved on. "But so far you've been chasing little squirts, just catching glances here and there, and you can barely keep up? Especially with all the naughty human kids running around, right?"

"And I suppose you can change all that," Jude said, slightly impressed despite himself. Inconvenience aside, it took serious guts to approach someone supposedly on a mission to eradicate one's species, even if Jude hadn't had all that much success so far. Still, he never would have thought to make first contact with a vampire, much less on its home turf. Even if this was some kind of trick, it was a daring one.

"Mm-hmm." Pixie nodded, still altogether too perkily for Jude's taste, or trust. "I know where they sleep."

Jude's skepticism and resolve wavered, but only for a moment. "The one I'm looking for is… something different than the ones I've seen around here."

"Different is good, makes 'em easier to find!"

"What, exactly, are you suggesting?" Jude asked, not at all sure he wanted to know the answer. But at least after he dismissed it he could go back to figuring out what to do with the vampire in his apartment and how to prevent it from being an issue again.

"A deal. I'll take care of your little monsters, if you take care of mine." Pixie smiled in a sly kind of way that reminded Jude of Jasper's cunning ringleader face, the one that said he was cooking up many schemes, behind many curtains. Coming from Pixie's comparatively much-more-innocent-looking face, it wasn't quite as convincing. "I scare away the naughty kids so you can focus on important stuff, like the nest of big baddies! Then you take them out, which is safer for everybody—we both win!"

"You're trying to get me to kill off others of your own… species?" Pixie shrugged, and Jude eyed him, looking for any hint of hostility or guile. He didn't find one, but that did nothing to reassure him. "Why?"

"Hey, vampires only turn into vampires because we get bitten and killed by other vampires. There's no weird loyalty system or whatever. I don't like these guys any more than I like… actually, I like you more than them. You're actually talking to me."

Jude considered the proposal, studying the young man's smiling face, pink hair, and complete lack of anything intimidating. Aside from that first flash of eyes and fangs, nothing about him was what Jude would call frightening, even to him, an unarmed and not-quite-able-bodied human. At all. "I don't know if you're up to this."

"Oh, come on, give me a little credit!" Pixie actually sounded insulted at the idea, defensive and eager to prove his undead prowess. "I can scare off a couple of bratty kids! It'll be fun!"

"That's not what I'm talking about. I'm not just out here hunting any random monster." Jude's tone dropped and expression along with it, frown deepening as he grimly remembered the initial reason for his five-year fixation. "There's one in particular."

"Huh..." Pixie nodded slowly as if to show he was following, and now he was the one giving Jude a cautious, searching look. "This one, uh, got a name?"

"No. No name, no face. Just claws, fangs and..." Jude shivered, remembering full moons and flames. "Fire."

"Well, that does kinda describe a lot of us," Pixie said thoughtfully, as if he were running through a mental roster of vampire names and reputations. Jude had to admit, such a thing might be of some use. "Even the fire part, more than you'd think. Most of us don't like it, yeah, but some of the bigger guys like to play with it, show off how badass they are."

"This one is responsible for more carnage than I can describe." Jude spoke slowly, tone full of warning, surprised to find that part of him hoped Pixie would listen. "It shouldn't have been possible. It *wasn't* possible. I've never seen anything like it and, somehow, I don't think you have either. This thing was... more."

"Hey, I'm still a vampire!" Pixie interjected, again sounding indignant. "I have fangs! And my eyes glow, and I can turn into a bat, and do all kinds of wild stuff! I'm—"

"Listen," Jude said in a much calmer voice than he would have expected from himself under the circumstances. "I'm sure you're great at...those things. But if I'm going to fight fire with fire, so to speak, I'm going to need something with a little more fire-*power*."

"Well, you'd be better off with me than throwing holy water that doesn't even work. And—*and!*" he continued before Jude could argue. "I saw you the other night."

"What other night?" Jude asked, instantly back on his guard. The more-than-slightly conspicuous Pixie had to have been watching for a few days at least and Jude hadn't noticed, even at his levels of hypervigilance and obsessive watch for threats. That was sloppy. Sloppy could get you killed just as easily as fangs. "Just how much have you been spying on me?"

"I haven't—okay, maybe I was spying, but just a little," Pixie admitted with a sheepish-looking shrug. "In the parking lot. You went up against two of 'em, they look like teenage girls? They're little, but they're nasty. And you totally froze up."

"I did *not*—"

"Dude, it's okay." Pixie grinned, fully revealing his two small front fangs for the first time. Like most things tonight, they weren't what Jude expected. Now that he got a good look at them, the little, only slightly-pointed nubbins were the opposite of threatening. If Jude wasn't so annoyed, apprehensive, and contemplating the most perilously bone-headed plan of his life, they might have been cute. "Scaring people's kind of their whole deal, and they've had about two hundred years to practice. They scare the heck out of me!"

Jude frowned and didn't answer. He didn't want to admit he knew the feeling, no matter how true. That would give away too much leverage, and that was the last thing he wanted a vampire to have on him, aside from fangs themselves.

"But yeah, you could use some backup," Pixie continued, apparently undaunted. "And I got you covered! Just remember, those girls can be creepy, but they're small fries. If you're after the big fish… follow me." He headed over to the window and casually brushed away some broken glass from the sill, which just felt insulting after what he'd done to it earlier. Then he turned back around to face Jude, meeting his hard, scrutinizing stare with an oddly optimistic look. "Just think about it, okay?"

Jude still said nothing. But he didn't reject the request either, painfully aware of his lack of any better alternatives.

"Cool! Good talk!" Pixie smiled again, this time fang-free. Without those, or the dramatic eye-flash, he looked like... somebody Jude probably would have still avoided like the plague. But definitely not as threatening as vampires were supposed to be. Jude just folded his arms tighter across his chest. The less monstrous this undead intruder turned out to be, the more confused he got. "See you later!"

There was no cloud of smoke or flash of light. One second Pixie was there, the next he just wasn't. Instead, on the windowsill sat a small, fluffy, familiar-looking bat. Very familiar. Very pink.

Jude and the bat regarded one another for a few seconds. It didn't move, just stared up at him with beady little eyes, and wiggling very large ears. Finally, feeling perhaps the most ridiculous he'd been this entire ridiculous night, Jude shook his head and spread his hands in a conceding gesture.

"I'll think about it," he said in as level and practical a tone he could manage while talking to a flying rodent. "But no promises."

Seeming satisfied, the small pink bat flopped the last couple inches out the broken window, dropped off the sill, and disappeared.

Alone in the silence, Jude stared at the mess of his apartment. Time to start putting the room, and his head back together. He'd start by sweeping up the broken glass. Tomorrow, he'd talk to Jasper about holy water and set a few related misconceptions straight. After he got a refund.

✺ XVI THE TOWER ✺

ACT THREE:
Pale Moonlight

JUDE EXPECTED Jasper to talk him out of it.

Not because he was a consistently cool head; that was Eva's department, and sometimes Jude's himself when it came to some of Jasper's more legally-ambiguous activities. It wasn't even a question of Jasper believing him. He knew vampires existed. They'd witnessed the same horror five years ago. But where Jude's coping mechanisms involved meeting horror head-on, Jasper's involved more evasion, more elaborate webs of intrigue. Even if Pixie had crashed into his window, Jasper was more likely to bury that fact along with so much trauma. He'd certainly tell Jude to do the same—and Jude almost found himself half-hoping for an excuse to back out.

"Well, I think you should see what he wants," Jasper said instead, not looking up from the same heavy book Jude had seen him with last. He'd read it throughout Jude's story and, by all appearances, seemed to find it more interesting. "And tell me everything, spare no detail."

Jude stared at him and his complete lack of concern or surprise of any kind. Somehow, even after all the borderline-absurd events of the past couple days, this was the strangest. "You actually want me to—what, form an alliance with the monsters I've been trying to hunt down all this time?"

"Doesn't sound like your new friend is one of those monsters in particular." Jasper finally glanced up at Jude before going back to studying the near-illegible writing on the aged, fragile page. No sequins this time. Today he was in all black, probably to go with the more occult leanings of his store. Even with the thick black eyeliner, it was relatively subdued compared to his usual finery and all that popped into Jude's head looking at him was 'beatnik poet.' Minus the beret. "But it does sound like this could be a mutually beneficial arrangement. I've made worse deals."

"Fine, but…" The store was empty, as usual, but Jude still had to lean in closer and say the next words in a near-whisper. "These are *vampires.*"

"Yes, they are!" Jasper finally closed the book and gave Jude his undivided attention. "And what do you do when a vampire comes along, offering you a once-in-a-lifetime opportunity?"

"Opportunity for what?" Jude scoffed, incredulous. No matter the angle he looked at it, all he could see was an annoying ex-neighbor and a pair of fangs, both much closer than he preferred.

"To know a vampire!" Jasper looked like he wanted to bop Jude's head with the book, but instead just stared at him, as if unable to believe anybody could fail to grasp this. "If somebody who isn't supposed to be real comes to you with the chance to learn everything you're not supposed to know—you take his offer! Who knows, you may find something you never knew you were missing. Can't judge a book by its cover. Or, in this case, a vampire by his fashion sense."

"I can't believe I'm hearing this." Jude said, bemused and still trying to wrap his overwhelmed brain around everything. And now this. "So if you were in my place, you'd just go with it and see what happened?"

Jasper smiled, and it looked genuine. Jude couldn't remember the last time he'd seen real happiness on his face. The thought left a subtle ache in his chest. "Like I said, I've made worse deals."

"Come with me, then." Jude spotted a ray of hope and went for it with everything he had. "I wouldn't mind getting into this mess so much if you were there."

"Why don't you ask Eva?" Jasper's smile turned a little teasing. "She'd be a lot better in a fight than me, anyway."

"Because you at least believe me." Jude said in a low voice, leaning forward to rest his hands on the counter between them. Unlike the last time he'd been in here, it wasn't a calculated move. No games this time, his request deserved to stand on its own. "And you know how important this is, more than anyone."

"Yes, I do." In response to his earnest words, Jasper met his gaze without a trace of mischief. "And I always believed. That's why I'm staying out of it."

"Are you serious?" Jude recoiled a bit, feeling as if the ground was shifting under his feet. He hadn't expected Jasper to want any part of it, but that wasn't what disturbed him. "You're leaving me to face all this alone?"

"I'm not leaving you." Jasper insisted, eyes hardening as if the idea were unthinkable, condemnable. "That will never happen. But some things are yours, just like there's a lot that's mine alone."

"I can't believe this," Jude said again, feeling any control he might have regained slipping out of his fingers again. "How can you tell me to do this, while you just sit there and 'stay out of it?'"

"Because I'm not you," Jasper said simply, with the serenity of complete conviction. "We're in different places, even if we're standing in the same room. We're trying to rebuild our lives, and that looks different for both of us. My life is here and has enough excitement in it already. And yours, I think, is about to get a lot more interesting."

Jude gave him a long, searching look. Despite all his friend's masks and evasions, Jude had never had a problem figuring out what he was actually thinking. Jasper had never made the habit of lying to Jude before, and he wasn't now, Jude felt that in his bones. "I thought you supported giving up."

"Giving up? No." Jasper said in a quiet but very certain voice. "Accepting the end of one life, and the start of a new one? Recognizing some things are lost, but still seizing hold of something else if it comes along? Jude, the man I was going to marry is dead. The life I was going to have is dead. I think that's true for all of us. I'm making a new life for myself but, until now, you…" He stopped, resolved expression softening again into one that was so warm and fond it made Jude's chest ache. "For the first time since I can recall, you look alive."

Jude shut his eyes briefly, feeling another, different kind of pang in his heart. "I don't really remember what that feels like."

"Maybe you can't tell, but I can." He heard the smile in Jasper's voice without looking. Some of the pain abated. "Walking death isn't a good look on you, Jude. This is a good sign."

Maybe when this was over, after he got some resolution, he might revisit living as opposed to bare survival… but there was still more going on here than met the eye, he knew that, if nothing else. With Jasper, things were rarely exactly as they appeared, even if no disguises were involved. "You know more than you're saying."

"Always," Jasper said, and Jude opened his eyes in time to catch the end of his casual shrug. "It's a universal constant by now. But it's nothing that would endanger you, that I do promise."

"So you really aren't coming with me?" Jude pressed. He could easily see the hesitation and uncertainty in Jasper's face and knew his resolve wasn't nearly as ironclad as he'd like Jude to believe.

"Ask me tomorrow." His black-lined eyes slipped away, as did any chance of solving that particular riddle. "I have… plans."

"Plans?" Jude repeated, not at all reassured by the non-answer. "Doing what?"

"Just some store security errands," Jasper said, an obvious evasion. So obvious, in fact, Jude got the feeling it was a hint for him to drop the subject.

"Well, that sounds ominous." Anyone else might have been talking about changing the locks or upgrading the metal shutters over the entrance, but Jude didn't think that was the case here. He wasn't even sure how much he believed about Jasper's supposed magic business, how much was real and how much was a distraction—but after what he'd seen the past two nights, he was starting to wonder.

"Not if everything goes according to plan." Jasper gave him one of his enigmatic smiles, the kind that made it hard to tell if he was joking and, if so, how much.

"All right," Jude backed off, hands raised. "I'll leave you to it. And don't worry, I *will* tell you everything. I blame you for about half of it."

"What?" Jasper actually looked surprised. "What in the world did I do?"

"That holy water." Jude gave him a dirty look before turning back toward the mall entrance. "Didn't exactly work as advertised."

"Oh." Jasper frowned briefly, but brightened fast. "Well, that's valuable information, anyway. Learning all the time!"

Shaking his head again, Jude left the store and kept walking, past the woman in black in her usual place outside. Some things never changed. She was still playing solitaire, still wearing dark sunglasses. Did she ever leave? All Jude wanted to do now was leave. Maybe he could actually spend a few precious hours at home pretending none of this had happened, and that all he had to worry about was keeping the mall safe and orderly for its human inhabitants.

As he stepped outside, however, that dream went up in smoke.

It was close to sundown, Oregon rain coming down hard, with clouds so thick the day was almost dark as night already. Still, vampires weren't supposed to come out in the daytime, no matter how cloudy. They were only supposed to appear at the stroke of midnight, emerging from shadows with fangs bared and eyes aglow like demons straight from Hell.

They definitely weren't supposed to stand there like they'd been waiting for him all day, wearing sunglasses, a black hoodie (like the shirt from last night, it read '*Chaos Chainsaw*'), red winter gloves, that same scarf, and holding a dripping umbrella overhead.

"Hey!" Pixie stopped mercifully before completing Jude's least-favorite joke, greeting, and song lyric, instead giving a smile and wave as Jude stopped in front of him. His face beneath the hood's shadow was as grey as the rainclouds overhead, but as long as he didn't open his mouth too wide, he could have been any other shopper.

"What are you doing here?" Jude had to ask, though he couldn't imagine a single answer he'd actually enjoy hearing. Pixie wasn't likely to be here for anybody else, much as he looked like he'd fit in with the goth store at the other end of the mall. Their employees tended to have the same kind of ridiculous, neon-fluorescent hair, and now Jude couldn't help wonder if they had pointed teeth in common too.

It was probably where he got the scarf in any case. At least now it looked like he'd finally taken off the tags.

"Waiting for you!" Pixie reached out, offering him space to stand under the umbrella, but Jude didn't move. "I've got something for us to start with. Wanna get going?"

"How are you here?" Jude asked instead, casting a confused look up at the sky. True, it was raining, and the sun would be down in an hour or so, but it was definitely still up behind the heavy cloud cover.

"Are you kidding?" Pixie returned, seemingly unperturbed both by the daylight and Jude's general lack of enthusiasm. "You're not exactly hard to find."

"No," Jude said, caught between exasperation and confusion. "I mean how are you standing here, in the daylight? I thought that…didn't work for you," he finished in a low voice, mindful of people passing by, but Pixie just laughed, nodding to his umbrella.

"Umbrella, hoodie, long sleeves—as long as there's some clouds, that's just about all you need, unless the sun actually comes out. Which around here really isn't much. Probably why you tend to see more of us in Portland than most places."

"Exactly how many of you are here?" Jude asked, interested in the answer despite himself. It wasn't even a strategic consideration now. He was undeniably curious, especially now that he couldn't help considering how many vampires he might have passed without knowing.

Pixie gave him the same kind of wry look that had reminded him of Jasper last night, when he smirked in the middle of a particularly good performance. Part of Jude found it annoying. The other part found it annoyingly endearing. "What, you think I know everybody in the vampire community?"

Jude paused for a moment, trying to decide whether Pixie was serious or not—though the look on his face gave the answer away fairly easily. Jude almost laughed, surprising himself and quickly turning it into a throat-clear. "I think that as long as...*you* exist, this is as good a place as any."

"Yeah. Especially if you *don't* technically exist. Keep Portland Weird!" Pixie grinned, just a brief flash of pointed teeth. "You should see the gang that hangs out under Powell's."

Jude wasn't entirely sure he should, so instead he fixed Pixie with what he hoped was an intimidating stare as he stepped under the umbrella, careful not to get too close, but not enjoying the idea of walking home in the rain. He tried to project the air of an experienced vampire hunter and not someone who still half-suspected that most or all of this was a particularly weird and elaborate dream. "I assume you actually have a reason for being here?"

"Not now," Pixie said, casting an anxious glance around he probably thought was subtle, but was anything but. "You have anywhere safer to talk?"

Jude had already done several things against his better judgement today. Now it was apparently time for one more. He started heading toward home and nodded for Pixie and his umbrella to follow.

Jude was halfway to his kitchen before he realized he wasn't being followed anymore.

"What are you doing?" he called, looking back to see Pixie still standing just outside the doorway, looking a little embarrassed but not actually entering the apartment.

"Uh, would you mind inviting me in?" Pixie asked with a nervous laugh, in which Jude didn't miss the undercurrent of anxiety. "It'd make everything a lot easier."

"So some vampire stories are true," Jude observed with only a faint sense of dismay at the directions his life had recently taken. At least it was nice to know he apparently had a choice in the matter, and Pixie was asking a good deal more politely than most humans tended to. He took a step closer, observing how Pixie's toes almost touched the door threshold, but not quite.

"Yeah, mostly the annoying ones." Pixie gave him a weak smile.

"You got in here last night." Jude frowned, recalling a shattered window and a near cardiac event, neither of which he was quite ready to let go. "I didn't invite you in then."

"You invited *somebody* in."

"I thought you were Eva—wait. That counted?"

"I guess?" Pixie shifted anxiously and shrugged, apparently no more familiar with the intricacies of vampiric consent than Jude was.

"That's cheating." One of the only upsides to any of this was that vampires had rules, long-established and almost universally recognized. Or so Jude had thought. The holy water had been the first hole in that theory and even this didn't seem to work in the way he'd predicted. Disturbing.

"Hey, we take what we can get. But yeah, keep that in mind," Pixie advised, a couple degrees more seriously. "Vampires like loopholes and most of us aren't as friendly as me."

Jude didn't acknowledge that. Instead he spent a few seconds weighing pros and cons, and wondering how private of a conversation they could have with his door wide open. Finally, he concluded that given the choice between being alone with a vampire in his apartment and neighbors overhearing anything he couldn't explain, he'd take the vampire.

"This is a one-time only invitation," he said, measuring every word to avoid ambiguity or wiggle room. "This is not a recurring arrangement. You do not drop by whenever you feel like it."

"All right, cool, whatever," Pixie said, folding his arms and shooting Jude the most sardonic look he'd seen yet. "Guess hospitality's reserved for the living."

Jude gave the look right back, complete with arm-fold. "You know, I could just leave you out in the hall and have you slip notes under the door."

Pixie looked chagrined, and his large ears drooped a little. "Sorry. May I come in, please?"

"Yes you may." Jude could swear Pixie looked relieved to actually cross the threshold without incident, as if he half-expected to be flung out of the room by a magical force. For all Jude knew, that might well be what happened to uninvited vampires. "Now what do you want?"

Pixie hesitated. Maybe he was picking his words carefully, just like Jude. Maybe the old 'they're more afraid of you than you are of them' saying applied to vampires as well. Pixie's attemptedly-casual tone when he finally spoke didn't fool Jude. He'd been in enough uncomfortable interactions to recognize when someone was trying too hard. "I found a way we could practice working together."

Jude folded his arms, not trusting this new ground for a second. They never had actually hashed out the details here. 'Working together' could have meant any number of terrifying things and he wasn't likely to enjoy any of them. "What kind of practice?"

"Don't worry, it's nothing dangerous!" Pixie smiled, flashing his small pointed canines at Jude. He seemed to be getting more comfortable showing them. Jude wasn't entirely sure if that was a good or bad thing. "Just scaring some kids, like we talked about. I mean, that's kind of your job, right?"

"Not exactly…" Jude hesitated, mildly astounded that he was even considering working in tandem with a vampire. This felt like a point of no return. After this first, real step, there would be no going back. "What did they do?"

Pixie's pupils dilated noticeably as his eyes narrowed, and, for the first time, a truly aggravated scowl spread across his usually-smiling face. "They stole my guitar."

Jude heard the missing guitar before he saw it. High-pitched noises like a distressed and wounded cat drifted from the empty parking lot ahead, where two figures stood under a streetlamp. It was a humid night, overcast and starless, just like before, when he'd cut through this parking lot and encountered a pair of fanged nightmares. The deja vu made him shiver, but he kept moving forward. It might be the same place, but this time would go very differently. These were kids, not monsters, and he wasn't going to collapse into a terrified heap.

"Do they have an amplifier too?" Jude asked, wondering if these kids had made off with anything more valuable than a guitar, maybe from the mall itself.

"They like taking my stuff, okay?" Pixie grumbled, more worked up with every step. Still not intimidating, however. Maybe this wouldn't be as terrible as Jude anticipated. Tonight might go a long way toward proving to Eva he was taking her, and his job, seriously. And, maybe, if he kept observing Pixie, he'd pick up some more useful tidbits on vampire wrangling.

Something spun and flashed beneath the streetlight. A lanky teenage girl was spinning on a skateboard barefoot, jumping and twisting to the discordant noise. Her ponytail of tiny, tight braids flowed behind her, and her skin shone a dark slate-grey under the light, a few shades darker than Pixie's. Jude recognized her with a chill—would have even without the curving shapes that flared from her shoulder blades. Wings.

"No…" Jude murmured. This wasn't going according to plan at all.

The smaller girl had the guitar. She also had short, spiked blonde hair and light grey skin. She wore a devilish smile as she picked at the strings, an awful screech emanating, as if she were playing it with very long claws. She was barefoot too, and every toe ended in a black, curved claw.

"Ugh, that's just offensive," Pixie groaned, mobile pointed ears pinned back tight against his head. "If you're gonna steal a guitar, at least have the decency to play it right!"

"*You're* offended?!" Jude said, more loudly than he'd intended to. The two undead teenagers weren't close enough to get a look at their fangs, but there was no mistaking anything else. "Those are vampires! You tricked me!"

"No! I navigated a tough situation with grace and efficiency!" Pixie actually sounded indignant, as if he was the one who had just been hoodwinked into creeping up on a pair of monsters.

"I thought you meant *human* kids!" Jude hissed as the pair of monsters stopped their playing and turned in their direction.

"Yeah... that was kind of the idea," Pixie admitted, as the girls set their stolen guitar down. The tall one kicked away her skateboard and it clacked against the streetlight behind them. Their eyes flashed blue-green. "I didn't think you'd help me otherwise!"

"Also cheating! Just like the window!" Panic made Jude's voice tight and he was overwhelmed with the urge to run. But instead of having no way out, his screaming brain was inundated with too many choices, none of them good. Bolt left? Right? Toward the closed mall, with its dark windows and locked doors? Back home, with the risk of bringing monsters right there? It was too much, everything was happening too fast, and Jude could hardly think.

"It was killing two birds with one stone!" Pixie fairly squeaked, sounding as scared as Jude felt. "And speaking of two birds—"

The vampire girls grinned and launched themselves toward their prey.

Jude stumbled backwards, but his back hit something—Pixie. They stood back-to-back, somehow in a stance that looked prepared instead of wildly accidental. "What do we do?"

"Just—try to look big!" Pixie raised his arms, his own eyes starting to flash the iridescent vampire warning sign. The girls seemed to further transform mid-run, fangs growing and faces warping into snarls. Their talons scraped audibly against the asphalt as the pair split from their straight-line dash and started to circle Jude and Pixie. The smaller one dropped down to all fours in an unsettling half-crawling run. "Get bigger than you are and make some noise!"

"That's *bears!*"

"I'm thinking, okay?" Pixie shot back. "Kind of expected you to know what to do here!"

"Me?!" Jude yelped, ducking and trying not to topple over as one of the creatures zipped by him so fast he felt the wind from her half-folded wings. "You're the vampire! You—"

He cut off as a familiar, deeply disturbing sound rose up from around them. High-pitched, eerie laughing. Laughter that, for the first time, became actual words.

"He never knows what to do with us," said the tall, thin one who'd performed graceful spins on the skateboard. She made a similar twirl past Pixie now, long black braids flying as Jude stared in combined shock and horror. Somehow he hadn't actually expected them to speak. "He's jealous. Can't blame him."

"Oh come on, Maestra!" Pixie sounded pleading and annoyed instead of outright afraid. "Just give it back, this isn't funny!"

"But you are!" The little one cackled, continuing to circle them in her crawl-walk, finger and toe-claws scraping loudly against the pavement. "Aren't you glad you're finally playing with us?"

"Stop it, Nails!" Pixie shuddered when she jumped into the air, spinning as if answering her friend's dance before landing in a very low crouch, elbows and knees bending in a way humans' never should. "That's *really messed up!*"

"Are those names? Do you know them?" Jude demanded, but just being able to form the question almost made him smile despite his alarm. He was terrified, facing down creatures of the night and probably death itself, but he wasn't overwhelmed, and he wasn't running. He was fully present in his terror, not flying into a panic attack or flashback. Baby steps.

"We've met!" Pixie wasn't trying to look big anymore. He'd lowered his arms and looked more frustrated than anything. "They think they're so cool, scaring the bejeezus out of everyone and taking my stuff without asking, couple of trolls! What'd I ever do to you guys, huh?"

"You're right," said the little blonde one, stopping her scrabbling circling and standing up to her full, not-overly-impressive height. But she didn't have to be tall to be dangerous—Pixie had called her 'Nails,' and considering her wicked-looking claws, it wasn't hard to see why. "We should totally chat."

"Like who's your friend?" said the tall, darker-skinned one. Maestra, if Jude had heard correctly. She exchanged a sidelong, smiling glance with Nails, and again Jude was reminded of his shock in this very parking lot just last night. They looked and sounded like normal teenage girls—just with more sharp points than usual. She grinned at Jude, and gave a twirl with more wings and claws than had to be strictly necessary. "Did he come back for more? Is he just dying to get dazzled again? Because that was fun."

"Again? Oh, you mean a couple nights ago? Is that the fun time you mean?" Pixie said, raising his voice before Jude could react. He jabbed a thumb at Jude and glared at the teenagers—even if they were actually centuries old, Jude couldn't help thinking of them as such. They certainly acted like bratty kids. "He was scouting you out. Letting you *think* you won, so he could, like, gauge your strength and fighting styles and stuff, and get the advantage. He's a *hunter*. And he's real tired of you tearing up his turf. I'd start running right now if I were you."

"Oh yeah, he's hardcore," Nails snorted, rising out of her deep crouch to put her hands on her hips. Somehow she stared down her button nose at Jude, despite being a good two heads shorter. "Looked real tough screaming and falling over, probably peed his pants when we—"

"Hey, he's not messing around this time!" Pixie retorted with a lot more conviction than Jude had in his entire body. "And neither am I! You guys went too far tonight. So just give back the guitar, quit scaring people, and nobody has to get hurt!"

"Pixie, *shut up*—" Jude started to whisper, but he was interrupted by another cackle.

"Seriously?" Maestra laughed, fangs flashing, and Jude took an involuntary step backwards. It was the same chilling, very inhuman sound from last night. Unlike her friend, she didn't hunch over, her movements were smooth and flowing instead of jerky and punctuated with contorted angles. She took another runway-model graceful step closer, long braids swinging, and a shiver ran up and down Jude's spine. "Is this supposed to impress us? Are we supposed to be shaking?"

"'Cause we're not," Nails finished before either of them could answer, looking at Jude with what he could only call amused incredulity, as if he were so pathetic it was hilarious. He couldn't remember the last time someone had looked at him like that, especially someone who didn't even look old enough to see an R-rated movie alone. But most teenage girls didn't have the lethality to back up their bravado and he fought not to take another step away. "He doesn't scare us and neither do you."

"Come on, Pixie," Maestra said in a more reasonable tone, though she still sounded right on the edge of laughing. "We were just having some fun with you. You didn't have to bring in a... *hunter.*" She said the last word as if it should have air quotes around it.

"That's not why I'm here," Jude blurted, finally finding his fear-twisted tongue, shooting Pixie a half-furious, half-panicked look. He hadn't planned on any of this, even if, in retrospect, he probably should have. He'd foolishly thought they were actually starting with something mundane and he was starting to think that even tangling with two relatively small vampires was an equally foolish idea. At the very least, they weren't supposed to talk. They weren't supposed to be kids who understood and answered him. They were supposed to be monsters. "I didn't know I was being dragged out here to *hunt* anyone tonight. All I know is that you have something that doesn't belong to you."

"Yeah, and we want it back!" Pixie seemed to have regained some confidence, though he'd never been as shaken up as Jude. "That guitar's mine. You don't even know how to play it, why do you want it?"

"Oh my gosh." Nails didn't even try to hide her giggle as she looked up at Jude, then away quickly, as if she couldn't look at him for too long before completely losing it. "If you wanted to hang out with us that bad, all you had to do—"

She stopped dead. The smile faded from her face in a split second, and her eyes, pale blue with the now-familiar vertical pupils, went very wide. They didn't flash in what Jude had come to understand as aggression, but she definitely wasn't laughing anymore. She held perfectly still, except for her flaring nostrils. Catching the way her friend had so abruptly frozen, Maestra turned to face Jude as well, looking confused. Beside her, Nails shook her head and jabbed one claw at Pixie. Immediately after an audible sniff, Maestra grabbed her by the arm and started to back away, suddenly looking about as scared as Jude had been last night.

"Yeah, that's what I thought!" Pixie laughed, standing up a little taller as they backpedaled. "You better run. Told you we weren't messing around here!"

But the gargoyle-like girls weren't paying attention anymore, having another of their whispered conferences and shooting definitely-disturbed looks Pixie's way. They seemed to have forgotten Jude was there at all.

"Well, that went even easier than I thought," Pixie said, sounding very satisfied as he shot Jude a grin. "See? No big deal. We can do this all night."

"What's wrong with them?" Jude asked, speaking for the first time and finding he needed to clear his throat. It had definitely started to close seeing the creatures so close-up, though he was still at least holding it together. Good. That was all he could hope for, really. "Why do they look scared of you?"

"Me?" Pixie looked at Nails and Maestra, then back up at Jude—and hesitated, seeming to slip back into the very careful, measure-every-word mode Jude had seen before. "Hey, you're the hunter here. They probably—"

"Thralls." Everyone froze at the sound of the harsh new voice. The word wasn't a shout, but it cut through the still night air like the crack of a whip. Beyond the streetlight's pale glow, a towering figure stood, silhouette a deeper black in the dark.

"No..." Pixie whispered. He took a step back so he was standing slightly behind Jude, then froze as if rooted to the ground by some unseen force.

"Pixie," Jude said in a low, very-carefully-reasonable voice as Nails and Maestra turned to face the newcomer, standing very straight. He could see the tension in their wings and shoulders from here. "We're leaving. Now."

But Pixie wasn't moving, or looking at Jude at all. He stared at the dark shape as it started to move closer, resolving itself into a tall, muscular man in a long trenchcoat. Pixie's mouth hung slightly open and his eyes were wide. They didn't flash, but the fear in them stood out, stark and palpable.

"Pixie," he said again, taking a step back as well, stopping when Pixie reached up to take hold of his arm. Jude didn't know exactly what he was doing, trying to hide behind him or steady himself, or maybe just make sure Jude was still there, but he held on tight as Jude struggled to form words. "Who?"

The answer was an even quieter, shaking whisper. One word, the foreign-but-familiar Latin syllables set off alarms in Jude's head. He knew that word, the same way 'transubstantiation' would forever be memorized, formative years essentially tattooing the rote knowledge across his brain. Even if he couldn't quite recall this word's meaning, images flashed through his increasingly panicked brain. Carved marble hands and feet. Metal nails, a cross, a face twisted in pain, or bowed in altruistic, agonized resignation. Flowing white cloth, bright red liquid. Wine or blood?

In the ringing of his ears, he heard a choir. Familiar and terrifying. Excruciating. Ex…

"*Cruce.*" By the time Pixie said it again, Jude could have whispered along with him. If he'd been able to move at all.

The vampire called Cruce was much larger than the two girls, Pixie, and most people Jude saw in his everyday life. He superficially resembled a man in his fifties, skin so white it almost seemed to glow under the streetlamp, cold and absolutely nowhere near lifelike. He stood at least a head and a half above even the taller of the young vampires, broad shoulders and thick-limbs reminding Jude more of a fighter's build than a vampire's expected litheness. His long, black trenchcoat swept the wet pavement, steel-toed boots echoing with every long, deliberate stride. With his shoulder-length grey hair, he might have been elegant, if he weren't bristling with so much raw hostility, fixing Pixie and Jude with a predatory stare. The way his large, black-gloved hands curled into fists made Jude's breath catch as painfully as if they'd been curled around his throat.

Cruce had the parking lot's undivided attention. Jude couldn't take his eyes off the intimidating figure long enough to glance at Pixie again, but heard him let out a soft, frightened whimper, the kind of noise Jude might have made himself, if he could speak or move at all.

The teenage vampires looked almost as scared, both holding perfectly still as Cruce reached them. He spared them a brief glance before fixing his white-gleaming eyes on Jude and Pixie.

Then his sharp command cut through the sudden quiet. *"Take them."*

But the two younger vampires looked up, sharing expressions of worry. "Why?" Nails asked, sounding completely lost and looking up at Cruce with a tilt of her blonde head. "Aren't we on the same side?"

"Kind of," said the taller one, Maestra, taking a step toward Nails with the same easy grace she'd had on her board, shooting a glance back toward Pixie. Oddly, now she looked almost afraid of him, conspiratorial in speaking to her cohort. "He smells like—"

Cruce made a fist, and they both fell silent. Instantly, they stood up ramrod-straight, staring at him with wide, unblinking eyes. All was still for a moment. Then his fist became a pointing finger, leveled directly at Jude and Pixie.

"Take them."

As one, the girls pivoted to face their targets, eyes flashing far brighter than they had yet, teeth bared and claws extended.

"Oh, crap," Pixie whispered, but it sounded distant. Everything did.

Jude couldn't move. He couldn't breathe. Pixie said something else, pulling at his elbow, but he couldn't bring himself to take a single step or look away from the monsters advancing on them. This was a dream. This wasn't real. Jude wasn't even sure if he was real himself.

It was five years ago, and the full moon shone bright overhead.

✸ XIII DEATH ✸

ACT FOUR: Flashbacks

FIVE YEARS AGO...

THERE'S FIRE on all sides but that's not what Jude is afraid of. It's under control. It's an intimidating blaze, but nothing they haven't dealt with before. It's familiar, even. And so is the place—he's been here before. They all have. The last time he saw it, though, it wasn't a construction site with newly-erected beams, it was a church. The last time they were here, Felix asked Jasper to marry him. It's surreal to see the change, even if the night feels the same, as if no time has passed. The moon is just as full and bright overhead.

But two things are strange. Wrong.

The first is that this fire shouldn't be here at all. The derelict building burned to the ground a month ago and in its place stands scaffolding—a new foundation, the bare skeleton of the project to come. Construction hasn't been completed, or even begun in earnest. There are no walls, no carpets, no insulation.

There's nothing to burn, yet fire blazes on every surface.

The second thing is harder to articulate. Jude is overcome with unease, not from being inside, with flames all around, but looking out. The walls are unfinished, so it's easy to see the dark sky and bright moon beyond. It's too clear, he thinks. The boundary between cool night air outside and the inferno in here is too perfect. It's like they're walled in with fire, neat and clean. It means something.

He doesn't have time to think what. Jasper cries out suddenly and Jude whirls in time to see something rush at him, something dark, indistinct, but horribly solid.

Jasper's head whips back like he's been shot in the forehead. Then he goes down, falling backwards in a graceful arc while his helmet flies in the opposite direction. The entire full-face mask has somehow been ripped clean off his head. He seems to hang in the air forever, but it's still too fast. He's on the ground before Jude can move.

Jude recovers quickly, world shrinking to Jasper falling. Nothing exists but this—not the fire and not the elusive, too-fast shape. He sprints as fast as possible in his heavy suit and helmet, scrambling across the uneven construction site ground to get to where Jasper lies, face-up but much too still.

Adrenaline slams through Jude's veins as panic threatens to overwhelm him. He calls Jasper's name, but gets no reply. Jasper doesn't move. Then Jude is on the radio, yelling for Felix and Eva, before it can fully hit him that Jasper isn't moving, and his eyes aren't opening. Jude frantically searches for his lost helmet, respirator mask, can't find anything, he has to work fast because he *knows* if he stops for half a second to think about this, he'll freeze, and they'll both be dead.

Where the hell is Eva? In a helicopter a mile out, far up in the sky. Jude has never hated their formation so much. And where is Jasper's goddamn helmet? It can't just be gone, the way *whatever-it-was* had hit him and disappeared, that didn't just happen, that was impossible too—

"*I'm coming,*" Felix says, voice loud in Jude's in-helmet radio, cutting through the roar of the fire and the static in Jude's head. "*Almost to you, just hold on. What happened? Is he all right?*"

"I don't know," Jude says desperately, even as relief floods through him at the sound of Felix's voice. He clings to it. He isn't alone here, help is on the way. "Something hit him, too fast to see what. Just one minute he's standing, the next he's down."

"Something hit him—you mean it fell? Room check, Jude. Do you think it's coming down?"

"No, no, not the building, something *in* the building with us!" Definitely on the edge of panic now. Jasper was hit hard enough to knock him out, helmet or no. Don't move people with head or neck injuries, Jude knows that, but what's the greater danger here? Possibly making the damage worse, or the definite threat of smoke inhalation? Jude takes a breath and tries to be coherent. "Felix, where are you? Jasper needs to get out of here, but I don't want to move him alone, I can't tell exactly where he's hurt!"

"Don't worry, Jude." Bless Felix. Bless his sweet voice and the way it eases Jude's clamoring mind when nothing else can. He's so scared it almost hurts, but he listens to Felix's voice, wraps himself up in it, and he can breathe. *"Everything's going to be fine. I'm right here and Eva's on her way. Just stay with him, please."*

"Yeah, yes, okay," Jude says immediately. He still can't tell what in the world hit Jasper but he forces himself to look up. Nothing else is falling or flying, the room looks stable, even if his brain keeps screaming that it *shouldn't* be on fire, nothing to burn, where is it coming from? Nothing feels real. "I'm not going anywhere."

"And neither am I. I see you!" Jude looks up to see Felix's suit-bulky silhouette framed in the space where a wall should be. No fire behind him, only the dark night sky. Jude's never seen anything more beautiful in his life. Weak with relief, Jude feels himself smile as he moves to carefully drape one of Jasper's arms over his shoulder. Felix will take the other one and they'll all be out safe in a minute. *"Hey, Jude."*

"Hey yourself." Felix is the only one who can get away with that. The only one who doesn't sound mocking when he does it, only ever warm. No one else is allowed.

Felix steps toward him and Jasper, bringing relief and rescue with every step. Jude's never been particularly lucky, but everyone gets at least one good thing in their life, and this is his. He's not alone.

Then he sees it. Felix doesn't. Someone is behind him, standing over his shoulder. Entirely calm amid the flames. Another *wrong thing* in a night full of impossible things going wrong.

Jude freezes, and so does his blood. Below his rising panic, he catches a glimpse of fangs.

"Felix," he starts, staring at the bizarre, incongruous, impossible apparition. He doesn't get to finish. Jude barely has time to register the deadly, needle-pointed canines and the curving, razor-edged claws glinting silver at the edge of the long, thin arms, before the creature is on him.

It moves in a blur. The attack is brutal, and lashes from the dark so fast his head spins. By the time Jude realizes what's happening, it's too late.

The first impact is to the center of his chest. Air rushing from his lungs, he staggers backwards. Then his feet leave the ground, and an iron grip latches around his ankle. Something stabs his calf, pierces through his reinforced suit, starts clawing its way up his leg. Before he can scream, a new, horribly sharp pain shoots from his knee down, up, everywhere. There is nothing but pain. It's white-hot, nauseating, dizzying, agony beyond anything he imagined his brain was capable of processing. It fills the entire world. It becomes him.

Under the pain and his own screams, he hears something rip. Maybe his suit. Maybe himself. Maybe he's being torn apart, skin from bone. Something slams into him from behind. The floor. He's on his back, staring up at the stars through a hole in the unfinished ceiling. Stars rush down to meet him— no. Eyes. Bright gold-gleaming, alien in their intelligent chill. The only thing he recognizes in them is a glint of laughter.

Just as suddenly, he's free. Whatever had its claws sunk into him is gone. The release is just as shocking as the stabbing torment.

He hears someone screaming his name.

Felix?

It doesn't matter.

It's not really happening. Nothing is real except pain.

Still, Jude struggles to sit up and look down. His leg is nothing. There's nothing below his knee but air. Blood pours out, turning the floor dark, slick, shining. Too fast. Bracing himself against a fresh surge of blazing agony, he curls around himself and clamps down on his ruined leg, but he might as well be trying to stop the bleeding with a Band-Aid. It's coming out much too fast, injuries like this, there's not much time. He knows it in a detached kind of way. He should be more upset, terrified, but even the pain is finally fading. Everything seems too far away to worry about.

Everything except for Felix standing in the middle of the room. His back is to Jude. Why won't he turn around and help? Did he see the shocking amount of blood and know it's already too late?

Felix is yelling something, Jude thinks, numb. He can't understand words anymore.

But the thing is still out there, the thing with the claws and fangs. He catches sight of golden eyes across the room and realizes Felix is standing directly between it and him.

The monster looks human. A man standing still, as before, calm amid the flames. Not one of them, no heavy suit. He's leaning a little to one side, head cocked under the wide brim of a hat, it looks like his hands are casually in his pockets. Jude wouldn't be surprised to hear a cheerful whistle. Instead, he dimly wonders how another person could do this to them. How it's even possible for someone to stand in the middle of a fire and not burn.

Jude never sees the man move. He sees him raise one hand, straight out from his body to point directly at Felix—but Jude never sees him rush forward. He moves too fast. One moment he stands across the room, the next...

His hand is sunk wrist-deep into Felix's chest. Like his hand is a blade, razor-edged, wickedly pointed claws puncturing Felix's suit, flesh, and bone.

It's impossible, Jude thinks as he watches Felix jerk to stand unnaturally straight upright, rigid with shock.

None of this should be happening. A man should not move in a blur through a fire and stab someone with his bare hand. It shouldn't be Felix and it shouldn't be like this. Jasper should be awake with them. Eva should be here. Jude doesn't understand any of this, but he knows *this is not how it was supposed to happen.*

The man rips his hand back out and it's almost as brutal as the stab in. Jude feels his own heart clench in response. His leg doesn't hurt anymore. All the pain has gravitated to his chest and it feels like his heart is shattering into a thousand tiny, sharp-edged pieces.

Felix falls.

He doesn't fly backwards like Jasper in an arc. Instead, his legs just collapse under him and he drops like a sack of bricks. Felix sprawls across the floor, long limbs bent at strange angles, thick-gloved hand landing so near Jude's face that, if he was just strong enough, he could reach out and take it.

Jasper is still unconscious, mercifully, behind him. Felix is worse than unconscious, he has to be. And Jude can feel himself slipping away, the edges of his vision going dark. It's only when his eyes sting and blur that he realizes he's crying.

The floor is a vertical horizon. Lost, spinning, Jude watches as black-and-metallic wing-tip shoes stride toward his face, like walking down a wall in zero gravity. Somehow, even amid the smoke, fire and blood, they're clean. With each step, he catches a flash of gold.

The man casually strolls over to where they all lie in a bloodied heap. Paying no mind to Jude's ever-weaker struggling, he bends down and grabs one of Felix's arms. Jude just has time to yell in protest, fighting to sit up and shove the man away, somehow keep Felix safe—when the man draws back his foot and then slams its sharp, gold-tipped toe into Jude's sternum, impossibly hard, hard enough that his suit's impact-resistant material feels like wet paper. Air rushing from his lungs, Jude falls backwards to the floor that's quickly growing slick with his own blood.

Jude only realizes Jasper is awake when he hears the anguished cries. Heart constricting, Jude tries to think, how long has he been conscious? How much horror has he seen? He's sobbing. Maybe words, maybe not.

Jasper tries to pull Felix closer, but the man kicks his arms away too. Then, as if a grown man and a heavy firefighting suit weighed nothing, the man—creature, monster, demon, *man*—pulls Felix directly out of Jasper and Jude's frantic reach, and lifts him clean off the ground.

"N...n..." Jude tries to cry out, but his throat is choked with tears, terror, and blood. He can't stop Felix from disappearing any more than he can stop the fire around them, not anymore.

He can hear thrumming high above and far away, like a rising storm reverberating across miles. Helicopter blades, Jude realizes faintly, and a smile pulls at the corner of his blood-caked lip. Eva is coming, flying to them as fast as she can. But not fast enough. She won't get here in time. Nobody will.

As his vision goes dark, a realization flashes into his mind. He knows what's been bothering him now, what's *wrong* with this entire scene. Fire where there's nothing here to catch. The impossibly neat divide between inside the burn and out.

The fire's perimeter is a perfect circle.

Jude almost laughs. He figured it out. He can't think anymore, but he knows. He's bleeding out and a monster just vanished, taking Felix with it, and Jasper is probably dying, and he'll never see Eva again, but he knows...

Nothing.

🔥

They rise up on all sides. A ring of stones, fingers of crystalline onyx reaching for a bright, clear sky. Jude turns around in the center, looks straight up into blue infinity. A perfect circle of black, shining obelisks. Like the fire. But this place is still.

Warm sand between his bare toes. The constant sound of crashing ocean waves.

A cool, salty breeze that raises the hairs on the back of his neck.

Bright blue-green water just outside the stone circle. It stretches in every direction, deep as the sky and just as endless. Gentle waves meet the soft, clean, white sand.

A peaceful, precious, too-brief, everlasting moment goes by before he sees it.

Somebody is lying on the beach, half in the water, half out. Not moving.

Jude doesn't hesitate. He rushes forward.

The person on the beach seems unconscious. Eyes closed. Shallow breath but regular, Jude notes as he carefully takes hold of their thin shoulders and pulls them onto dry, warm sand. Long, straight black hair trails on the beach, in the water. Their sleeping face is pale, almost grey, and they burn with fever. Their skin is dry.

He doesn't recognize their androgynous features. But it almost feels like he should. Like he's missing something. This face isn't familiar, but it's *important*.

A black mask rests on the sand beside them and Jude thinks of his respirator face mask. Jasper's, impossibly taken. This one has no plastic tubes, no purified air tank connected. Instead it has a long, gracefully curving shape, like a water bird's beak. There's something important about this strange, bird-face mask too. He knows it, the way he knows its owner is… not *familiar*. Not yet. Significant.

Jude doesn't know them yet, but thinks he might.

He turns back to the unconscious person on the beach beside him; is their breathing easier now? Their white dress is rough, fabric uncomfortable to the touch. The edges of their long skirt are ragged, singed black as if they've been burnt, and impossibly dry after being pulled from the ocean.

He freezes, remembering fire.

But before he can move or say a word, the almost-familiar stranger opens their eyes. Black and shining as the stones around them, and quick, locking onto his face without a moment's hesitation. They look up into Jude's eyes, and for one moment, it's like seeing his own reflection. There's a strange recognition in their dark eyes, the same kind he feels, not of knowing, but connection. Of *yes, this is important. Yes. Remember this. Yes.*

When they speak, Jude doesn't understand the words. But he hears the anxiety in them. Their voice is tight with desperation, and the scared-sounding syllables go over his head. He doesn't know what language. One he doesn't speak.

"I'm sorry," Jude says, and deeply feels it. Why is he so painfully aware that this is a crucial moment, but not what makes it so? Why does he know he's missing life-altering details, but not what they are? He can feel the not-stranger's hands clasping his own the way he feels the sand, the water, the breeze. It's the most tangible, vital, real thing he's ever felt.

"No..." They frown, and he watches as they shift from disturbed disorientation to realization. They must feel it too, that this isn't right. This isn't how it's supposed to be. When they speak next, it's slow, halting, as if the translation is hard work. But this time Jude understands. *"Is he all right?"*

Someone else asked him that not long ago, he remembers dimly. Jude didn't know the answer then. He doesn't know it now. And he doesn't have time.

In a moment, the beach, the circle of stones, the sky, and the person with the mask are gone, and he is somewhere else.

🔥

The first thing Jude feels is pain. He's aware of it before anything else, keeping his eyes closed while sensation worms its way into his consciousness. Why does it hurt? He won't find out like this, so he blinks a few times, and the first thing he sees is a harsh white light.

He immediately shuts his eyes again and gasps in a breath that burns in his lungs. He remembers seeing the bright, full moon overhead, Felix's screams reverberating in his ears. If the moon is here, then...

He's warm but not burning. There's no hard ground under his back. The air he sucks in doesn't taste of acrid smoke and metallic blood. It's cool, with a sharp, antiseptic edge. There are no screams. Instead, a regular beeping comes from somewhere near his head. He holds perfectly still for another moment, then slowly opens his eyes again.

A bed. Four white walls, white ceiling. A fluorescent light overhead, not the full moon. His breath returns, much more slowly. Still, everything hurts and his throat burns with a terrible thirst. It feels like he's been dropped from a dizzying height, every bone in his body rattled and sore. The pain centers in his left leg, sharpens, resolving itself into a wave of nausea that washes over him as his vision clears.

Jude struggles to move his head, straining to see more of this room than the too-bright ceiling. He fights to sit up and look down at his leg. But what he sees next shatters any slow-developing thoughts and makes his breath catch in his dry, aching throat.

He's not alone. Jasper is in a chair beside him, but half-lays face down on Jude's bed, resting his forehead on both his arms. His breathing is shallow and slow, as if he's fallen asleep. There's a hand on Jasper's back, moving in a slow, endless circle. Eva's, Jude realizes, and slowly looks up at her face. She's standing next to the chair and bed, but her eyes are closed. She looks asleep on her feet, dark circles under her eyes and fatigue etched into every line on her face.

Felix is nowhere.

Jude lets out a small groan as he struggles half upright, and that's enough to get attention. Eva opens her eyes first, glancing down at Jasper as if thinking he'd made the sound—then her gaze snaps to Jude's half-awake face, eyes widening in what looked like combined shock and joy.

"Jude," she says, the whispered name coming out on a rush of air, as if she'd been holding her breath. "You're awake. He's awake," she says, a little louder. Her hand, which had stopped as the rest of her froze, went back to rubbing Jasper's back, harder this time, to gently bring him back to the present.

Jasper slowly raises his head and looks up, bleary-eyed as if he really had been asleep. It takes a couple seconds and blinks for joyful recognition to flash across his face, and light up his tired, red, raw-looking eyes.

"Hi," Jude manages to say, a smile starting to pull at the corners of his mouth. He's happy, bizarrely. So happy just to be here, to be alive and have them near him, no matter how much it hurts. He wants to stay in this moment forever.

"*Hi!*" Eva laughs, or maybe sobs. He can tell that she's smiling, even as her shoulders start to shake.

"We thought we'd lost you." Jasper's voice is raspy and just above a whisper. For the first time, Jude notices the white bandage around his forehead, partly hidden by his uncombed hair. He remembers an impossibly-fast, dark shape flying through the air to slam into Jasper's head with an awful *crack*. But Jasper's alive, conscious, safe. And now his hand lifts from the bed and reaches for Jude, as if he wants to touch his face. But he stops, wavering—and Jude doesn't have the energy to lean forward as he wants to, so badly. Instead, Jasper's warm hand slips around his, and he gives it a weak squeeze.

"Welcome back." Eva says, looking exhausted, worn bone-ragged, but whole. The tears shining in her eyes must come from relief, because he can see the tension and worry melt from her face, feeling his own disappear with it. He knows that smile. He knows everything is all right now. "Glad you made it."

"Me too." For a moment, he thinks of nothing but this, nothing but the three of them, and lets his body lay down again, feeling heavy, sleepy and warm, relief flooding him. Then something occurs to him and the flash of anxiety shakes away any lingering sleepiness. He's awake, alert, and the growing nausea that comes with consciousness makes him wish he wasn't. But he still needs to know. He needs to know why the three of them aren't four.

"Felix?" Jude asks, trying to prop himself up on an elbow to see the doorway out into the brighter-lit hall. Nobody answers, and cold fear starts to seep into his heart again. He looks up to see the relief freeze on Eva's face. Her eyes flick down to Jasper and Jude's follow. Jasper isn't looking at him. He's not really looking anywhere.

"How much do you remember?" Eva asks quietly, and now she looks apprehensive, like she's about to venture out on very thin ice, praying not to see cracks.

"I..." Enough. Jude remembers enough. He sees Felix fall, like it's happening right now, clawed hand like a dagger piercing his heart, his willowy body sprawling across the ground. He hears a strangled scream and sees Jasper struggle to pull Felix's limp body into his arms. He sees a dark shape come up behind them. And here, now, a cold, sharp weight of fear settles in his stomach. He starts to shake. When he speaks again his voice trembles, like the rest of him. "Where is he? Is he all right?"

It's only after he says the words that Jude realizes he's heard them before. In a dream of the beach and the strange, long-haired person on it. Is this how they'd felt then? Desperately searching Jude's face for a reason to hope, the way he's watching his friends now?

Slowly, anything like hope vanishes from Jasper's face, leaving behind something Jude never wanted to see there. Something hollow. Broken. Stripped, as if every bit of life has been torn mercilessly away, nothing remaining but bones. Like the construction site's metal scaffolding silhouetted against the night sky and flames, the unfinished building going up in smoke. The bed is warm but he feels cold.

"No," Jasper whispers, though Jude doesn't need the answer anymore. He doesn't want to hear it, but he hears it anyway. "He's not."

Five years later, the moon was full again. And, again, Jude was frozen in horror.

Immediate terror and remembered agony rooted him to the parking lot pavement and his knees shook, threatening to buckle under the crushing weight of trauma and unanswered questions. Everything came back in a rush, everything he'd tried to bury and forget so he could function, everything he tried to pretend he was over and done with, the past he pretended was past, even as his present and future crumbled.

"Take them."

Cruce's words floated back, and Jude realized that what felt like hours of terrified memories must have only been a few seconds. The imposing vampire was still pointing one black-gloved finger in his direction, ordering the two vampire girls to attack—but no, not directly at him.

Jude felt something press against his shoulder and realized Pixie was still there. He hadn't run away. They were standing back to back again. They both might still die in the next minute, but he wasn't alone and that was something, more than Jude expected. The thought was a grim comfort as the pair of girl-shaped creatures of the night came flying towards them.

They moved so fast Jude could barely keep them from becoming windswept blurs. As they had before, they sped around Jude and Pixie like they were trying to whip up a tornado in the parking lot. Before, they'd let out keening shrieks and hair-raising giggles, but now they were silent and that was worse. Jude was afraid to move and terrified to stay still. If he moved they'd attack for sure, and if he stayed still, he was just waiting for the first strike.

But then, the pair leaped back, putting about thirty feet of distance between themselves and Jude and Pixie. They exchanged a glance, and seemed about to charge again with a running start—when they stopped moving forward. Then they stopped moving at all, except to reach out to take each others' hands.

"What are you waiting for?" Cruce snapped. "Get him!"

But the girls held perfectly still, together hand in clutching hand, like the contact was the only thing keeping them standing straight and tall. They remained about halfway between Jude, Pixie, and the towering Cruce, who hadn't bothered to take another step. Behind them, their leader let out a wordless snarl of fury, black-gloved hands curling into tight fists. Even from here, in the low light, Jude could see his bright eyes narrow into a glare. And Jude couldn't move an inch, frozen just as fast as the two teenage vampires seemed to be.

"Fine. I'll collect him myself," Cruce said in a harsh voice that made Jude's stomach feel like it was being squeezed in a cold, tight grip.

"*Run!*"

At the sound of Pixie's voice, a sudden burst of wind rushed by Jude's face, followed by a rapid flapping noise from behind him. He whirled around, expecting to see Pixie running, but there was nothing there but dark parking lot. Pixie must have taken the easy way out, the smart way, and left him here to face these monsters by himself. Panic rising, Jude turned back around, and immediately ducked—the huge vampire in the long black coat was closer than before, closer than he should or *could* possibly be, too-bright eyes flashing in the dark.

Jude almost overbalanced and fell to the ground, but managed to keep on his feet as he scrambled backwards. Every instinct, both natural and learned, screamed at him to run, hide, never look back, leave everything behind him, now and for the rest of his life—but he didn't, even as he fought with himself to *do the smart thing and run,* just like Pixie had. The girls were still standing where they'd stopped, and he had the strangest feeling that they were every bit as scared of Cruce as he was.

Cruce didn't pursue him either. He was looking up at the sky, hands raised as if to snatch something from the air. If Jude ran for it now and kept running, was there a chance he could make it to safety before they realized he was gone?

Collect him, Cruce had said. He knew Pixie, just like the other two. They'd never been after Jude at all.

Jude felt a surge of relief, but panic quickly followed. He barely had time to hope Pixie had gotten away when he caught a flash of bared fangs and any power he had to move dissipated instantly. *No, no, no,* Jude thought frantically and he could *feel* himself start to freeze again, joints locking in place as terror overwhelmed him and pain, current and remembered, shot through the spot where his knee sat in his prosthetic. Why now? Out of every frustrating, inopportune time he'd run into a wall of panic and memory and felt his body and brain grind to a halt, this was the worst. He had to run, he had to move, yell for help, *do*—

Something flew into Cruce's face. Something with small but furiously flapping wings, letting out a barrage of fast, high-pitched screeches.

Cruce swore, stumbling back a step and reaching up to shield his head with his arms. Jude caught a glimpse of pink and realized the bat currently dive-bombing Cruce's head wasn't a bat at all, or wasn't always at least. He barely had time to register the relief, actually feel himself smile, when one of Cruce's large hands shot up, seizing the Pixie-bat from the air.

"Let him go!" Jude yelled, words out of his mouth before he'd consciously formed them. Stricken, he watched as Cruce's head slowly turned toward him. The vampire's face twisted in a terrifying grimace, long fangs bright and eyes flashing brighter than before, glowing instead of just reflecting the light. Jude couldn't breathe.

Without warning, Cruce's fist flew in a blur, hurling the bat through the air and sending it slamming to the ground. It hit the pavement with an awful thump and a short, sharp *squeak!* before falling silent and much too still.

That small sound was enough to shake Jude out of his horror, and rush forward. Thankfully, Pixie had been flung some distance away from Cruce, and Jude didn't stop running as he stooped to scoop the small bat up as carefully as he could.

Run. Run where? He thought as he scrambled toward the edge of the parking lot and the lights beyond. Could you even run or hide from vampires? He couldn't go back to the dark, locked mall, and he shouldn't go home and risk bringing these creatures right to his doorstep—to Eva and Jasper—but he had nowhere else. Home at least had doors, thresholds they couldn't cross without permission. They wouldn't be able to follow him in, if Pixie was to be believed.

And since Pixie was currently a scared, shaking bat in his hand, injured after protecting him, Jude found it a lot easier to believe him than expected.

He turned toward the lights and charged for them with everything he had, only realizing there was something on the ground in front of him when he almost tripped over it.

A guitar.

Remembering his promise to Pixie but not slowing down for a second, Jude reached down to grab it up too. It was much heavier than he expected, almost sending him crashing to the ground. Thankfully, he managed to stabilize long enough to get his feet back under him, and avoid crushing the bat who'd burrowed deeper between his hand and chest.

A terrible howl came from behind him and fresh adrenaline surged through his veins. Cruce sounded furious at losing his prey. But then two more shrieks cut through the air, higher-pitched but just as chilling. He shot a glance over his shoulder long enough to see the two smaller vampire girls snap into motion again—but not in pursuit. They rushed between Cruce and Jude, trembling but blocking the way long enough for Jude to get a few more precious steps away. They were still holding hands, as if separating would break them.

Jude felt a pang of guilt and almost wished they'd follow him and keep running. He'd never feel good about leaving teenagers alone with a man like Cruce. But these teenagers had claws and fangs, and Jude had a guitar and an injured bat.

Holding Pixie as close as he dared, Jude sprinted for the bright windows and safety of his apartment building, and tried not to look back.

Jude made it all the way to his building, up the stairs, and down the hall before he realized they weren't being pursued. The corridor was silent. Nobody chased them up the stairs or burst out of the elevator to attack them. Outside, the night seemed calm and quiet. Jude stopped outside his door just long enough to catch his breath before digging for his keys, awkwardly setting the guitar down on the floor and trying to hold onto the fuzzy, limp bat in his other hand.

He got the door open and was about to rush inside when Pixie gave a strenuous wiggle in his hand, flapping his wings until Jude let him go, startled. The pink bat flopped to the ground, but by the time he hit, he wasn't a bat anymore. As before, there was no sound, flash, or any other sign of transformation. Just one second a feebly wiggling bat, the next a human-sized Pixie slumped on the hallway carpet against the wall, head hanging down and looking barely awake.

"What are you doing?" Jude demanded, throwing frantic glances up and down the hall. It was empty and, if someone entered now, all they would see was him, a guitar, and Pixie sitting on the floor, dazed.

"Can't come in," Pixie said faintly, and Jude had to bend down to hear better.

"What? Why can't..." He stopped, watching as Pixie weakly extended a shaking hand to point at the open door to his apartment.

"Gotta ask me."

"Oh my God," Jude muttered, briefly shutting his eyes. This night kept switching from absurd to terrifying and back again. Right now seemed a little of both. "I have to invite you in, specifically?"

Pixie didn't answer, just gave a little nod and let his head tip back against the wall.

"Okay! Fine!" Jude said, reaching down to grab the guitar, pull Pixie to his unsteady feet, and keep the door from shutting with one of his own, the one that only screamed in phantom pain. "Yes, come in, just stay with me!"

Evidently this was enough, because they made it over the threshold without incident. Jude set the guitar down against the wall and half-carried, half-dragged Pixie over to his couch, dropping him as gently as possible. Pixie immediately shut his eyes and lay down, as if he was going to take a nap right there. Blacking out might be more accurate, Jude thought, feeling a familiar and unwanted surge of raw, incoherent panic.

What would he do if Pixie actually collapsed in his apartment? Jude wasn't about to kick him out, but what did you even do for an injured vampire, short of opening a vein? He had no way of knowing whether first aid or anything potentially helpful for a human would do any good here. Jude almost wanted to call Eva or Jasper for help—but how in the world would he explain this? Any of it?

Jasper knew. About vampires, about magic, probably more than Jude did, all things considered. But he'd also said in no uncertain terms that he didn't want to be involved, and Jude couldn't bring himself to reach out now. Jasper would help, he was sure, but Jude had to at least *try* to fix this on his own, he owed him that much and more.

That left Eva. But he couldn't call her in the middle of the night babbling about vampires, they'd barely made peace the last time she was here, when she gave him all of the—

Jude practically ran to his fridge and yanked it open, grabbing the red bottle of blood-infused steak sauce and hurrying back to Pixie.

"Here—drink." Jude said, shoving it into Pixie's hand. The vampire actually looked so weak it was a wonder he didn't drop it, and he peered at the bottle blearily.

"Whuzz…" he mumbled, blinking as if the label were difficult to read.

"Steak sauce," Jude explained, fully expecting Pixie to fall unconscious right in front of him. "It's got blood in it. I don't know how much, or if you need it raw or something, but it's worth a shot."

"Mmkay," Pixie said, still sounding about three-quarters out. For a moment Jude wondered if he should open it or if Pixie would be able to do it himself—but Pixie unscrewed the cap with shaking hands and raised the bottle to his mouth.

The change wasn't dramatic. Jude expected Pixie's eyes to flash again, or some kind of inhuman screech, maybe for him to sprout giant wings—but none of that happened. Pixie didn't even drink very fast. Instead of pouring it down his throat, he took very slow, hesitant sips. His biggest reaction was a few quick blinks as he took another look at the label before continuing to carefully drink. It was all much less…bloody than Jude expected, but then, not much about Pixie had met his admittedly horrifying expectations.

After a few seconds, Pixie gave Jude a questioning look that almost looked like he was searching for approval. Jude automatically gave him a nod, and that must have been reassuring enough for Pixie to take a couple more tentative sips. When he did, Jude let himself relax and slumped forward, resting his forehead in the palms of his hands. The night had been exhausting, and he wasn't even the one who'd come close to collapsing.

For a while, they sat in silence, Pixie taking small, careful mouthfuls and looking at the bottle as if deep in thought, and Jude sitting with his elbows on his knees, face in his hands.

"Thank you," Pixie said after around five minutes and, when Jude slowly looked up, he saw an expression he didn't expect. Pixie was watching him with wide eyes, filled with something that might be tentative hope. "This is really good. I definitely needed it."

"Don't mention it," Jude answered, entirely sincere in the hope that Pixie wouldn't. "What happened back there? Who was that?"

"Cruce," Pixie said faintly, voice dropping to just above a whisper. Jude didn't like the look on his face, mixed fear and absolute exhaustion. "A bad guy. Really bad."

"One of the tough vampires you expect me to be able to deal with?"

"Can't blame a guy for hoping." Pixie gave him a joyless smile and sighed, looking like he might fall asleep right there on Jude's couch. But his heavy-lidded eyes stayed open, and he took another careful sip of sauce. "But he's something else. A lot worse than his little mind-controlled minions, anyway.

Poor kids."

"That's what happened to them?" Jude asked with a shiver, remembering the way Nails and Maestra had snapped to attention, how it had seemed like they were fighting back toward the end.

"They're called thralls," Pixie mumbled, voice flat and appropriately lifeless. "Whenever a vampire turns someone, they form like this... bond. It's supposed to be a good thing, I guess, if you're tight and trust each other and stuff. But if you get turned by an asshole? Good luck. They get to walk around in your head whenever they want. Make you do whatever they want. It's..."

He trailed off, and Jude almost didn't want to pursue this admittedly terrifying subject, but he had to know. "Could he do that to you?"

"Cruce? No," Pixie said with a weak shake of his head, but he didn't seem very happy about the answer. If anything, he looked even more like he wanted to burrow into the couch and hide until everything was over and the world made sense. Jude wouldn't have minded that himself. "No, he didn't kill me, someone else... I'm not one of his, that's all."

He fell silent again, and this time Jude didn't push any further. After a few seconds of silence, he changed the subject to another burning question. "So, does that taste better or worse than plain blood?"

"Better, definitely," Pixie said, taking another sip with an appreciative look, seeming a little relieved at the conversation's progression. "But I haven't really... I mean, I don't know for sure, exactly."

"You don't drink blood?" Jude stared at him, realizing that in all the chaos, he'd never actually thought to ask.

"Not if I can help it." Pixie set the bottle down, still looking a little shaky, but his eyes were clear and his movements steady. Still, he didn't meet Jude's eyes, and his usually-expressive voice was uncharacteristically flat. "I mean, does drinking blood sound like fun to *you?*"

"Only in sauce form," Jude said, and Pixie looked up as if expecting to see him smiling. But Jude was still processing, not laughing. "If you don't drink blood, then how do you…"

"Stay alive? So to speak?" Pixie leaned back, looking up at the ceiling. Jude didn't quite believe his casual tone, and the troubled look in his eye further betrayed it. "Well, I know we need to drink. Feed. Whatever. Especially when we get hurt, like, uh. Just now. But there has to be like, a minimum, right? Drink as little as possible, but still survive and be able to think and function and stuff? Guess I'm trying to figure out what that is."

"You're talking about basically starving yourself," Jude said, eyebrows coming together. He couldn't help the undercurrent of concern that made it into his voice. "That can't be the best option."

"Hey, people who will willingly let me chomp their neck or arm or whatever, they're few and far between." Pixie didn't sound overly worried about this, resigned if anything. "And I'm not gonna do it if someone doesn't say I can."

"That's… good." Jude's brow furrowed a little more. Something about this wasn't right. Blood wasn't food, and it wasn't starvation, exactly, but vampires still needed it to survive. Going without meant constantly running on near-empty, scraping the bare minimum. Had Pixie been on the edge of collapse this entire time? He did a good job of hiding it, but if his exhaustion now was any indicator… "Is it like coming into a building, you can't do it without permission?"

"Nope, we can bite whoever we want," Pixie said, taking another sip and looking at the red bottle with increasing appreciation and energy. "I'm just not a douche."

Jude couldn't help but feel relieved, seeing Pixie actually drink—feed?—without the obvious shame or fear he otherwise felt. But Jude couldn't find a way to express this that didn't sound… he didn't even know what. He was just glad they seemed to have found a solution, at least for now. Somewhat reassured, he sat with Pixie in a silence that wasn't anywhere near as awkward as he'd expected. He didn't watch him drink, something about it felt personal. Instead he rolled up his left pants leg in slow movements and busied himself with his prosthetic, readjusting it in a vain attempt to ease the ache in his knee and thigh.

"So, um… You kinda froze up again back there," Pixie said after a little while longer, giving Jude a careful look. His gaze wasn't accusing, but it was curious.

"I know," Jude said, looking to Pixie just before his eyes dropped to the floor. "I'm—I'm sorry."

"What happened?" Pixie asked, eyes going to Jude's prosthetic leg, and then flicking back to his face and staying there. Jude had expected that. Whenever it was remotely visible, new people tended to get thrown for a loop, and never knew where to look. It was always awkward—for them, since Jude had long since stopped caring, wishing people would just ask whatever too-personal question they needed to get out of their system, so everyone could move on. Fortunately, Pixie didn't seem about to go that direction. He had other annoying questions to ask. "Like, I know you get freaked out seeing vampires, but you're a hunter, right? You have to have done this before at least a little."

Jude almost retorted. He wanted to snap that Pixie should mind his own business, that if he was so smart and knew how to fight without slipping into paralyzing terror or overwhelming panic, he should do it himself and leave Jude in peace. But he didn't. He wasn't even angry, only drained. And telling the truth might not be pleasant, but it was easier than keeping up the distance. "I've never… done this before, no. I *want* to. But flashbacks don't make it easy."

"Flashbacks? Like P.T.S.D.?"

"Not 'like' P.T.S.D.," Jude said, just above a mutter. "I know exactly what's going on in my brain. I can feel it coming, I know what's happening, but I can't stop it. It's… very frustrating."

"Yeah, but at least you know what's going on," Pixie suggested.

"Whoever said knowing was half the battle—"

"G.I. Joe?"

"Well, they're wrong," Jude said, rubbing at his temples. "It doesn't make it any easier."

"Does talking about it?" Pixie didn't withdraw when Jude looked up sharply. "I'm guessing you don't do that a lot."

"No, I don't," Jude said after a few deep, considering breaths. "None of us do. It's easier that way."

"Well," Pixie said, a little hesitantly but looking oddly optimistic, like he'd just hit on a good idea he was excited to share. "You can talk to me if you need to. Or want to. Hey, it's not personal with me, right? We're just working toward the same things. It's just sharing stuff so we're on the same page, and we can get stuff done as easily as possible, right?"

"Not personal?" Jude repeated, surprised at the tentativeness in his own voice.

"Nope." Pixie shook his head. The sauce looked like it had done him some good, his warm brown eyes were brighter and even his large ears looked a little perkier. "Just business."

"It was…" Jude struggled to find the words. Even recall with no intention of sharing was overwhelming, and he tried to actively remember as little as possible. It seemed more like a force of nature, however unnatural. The chaos, agony and fear in its wake were more powerful and deadly than any uncontrolled burn he'd ever seen. While he tried to find the words, Pixie drank more of the sauce, face slowly beginning to lose the unhealthy pallor. On anyone else, Jude would say the 'color' started to return to his cheeks, but here that color was only dark grey.

Haltingly, voice hollow, he told Pixie what he remembered of the full-moon night his life had changed completely, and Felix's had ended. Almost everything he remembered. Jude kept the more excruciating pain to himself. Some things were sacred.

"I'm sorry," Pixie said at last, when Jude's story was finished and he was around halfway-done with the bottle of sauce. He sounded somewhere between horrified and awed. He didn't know what to say, Jude knew. Nobody ever did. Most nights, even he couldn't wrap his own head around any of it. "And I know that doesn't mean anything, really. Nobody can really understand something like that until they live it, right?"

Jude opened his mouth, but instead of replying, folded his arms and looked at the floor. Some points he wasn't ready to concede. "I close my eyes, and every time, I see fangs. Nothing stops the nightmares. Hell, even back then—I *died!* My heart stopped for sixty seconds. You'd think it would be over then, if nothing else. But it wasn't, and I can't forget what I saw then, either. Even death wasn't enough."

"At least that part wasn't as terrible as the rest of it," Pixie said, in a tone that clearly meant he was trying to find a nonexistent bright side. Jude had no patience for it, or anything else that masked reality. "I mean, if you're gonna almost die—"

"I did die," Jude maintained, feeling oddly defensive. "Temporarily, but I died."

"Well, I died too," Pixie said, and Jude shut his mouth, breaking off his automatic retort. It was the way he said it that hit harder than the actual words; plain, simple and inarguable. "And I didn't see anything like that. At least you got something."

"No, I didn't. It wasn't Heaven," Jude said, but there was no fire in his words, only exhaustion. "And that burned person wasn't an angel. They were an aggregate my subconscious made up of everyone I've ever pulled out of a building on fire. It was my oxygen-starved brain calling up old memories while it broke down."

"How do you know, though?" Pixie pressed, with the slightest edge of desperation. "Five years ago you didn't believe in vampires. A couple days ago, you didn't think you'd ever have a conversation with one. What are you gonna believe in tomorrow?"

"If there was any justice in the world, none of this would have—" Jude broke off and took a slow, deep breath. When he spoke it was at a normal volume, not the near-shout he'd started without realizing. "Do you know what was left of Felix after that thing was done with him?"

"No," Pixie said in a small voice, sounding afraid to hear the answer.

"Enough to bury, but that's it. He wasn't recognizable. There were human remains all over that construction site—homeless people caught inside, they said. Most so badly burned that all they could tell was the DNA was human."

"So then... if there was no body, and no DNA evidence for sure—"

"There was blood. Too much for a person to lose and survive. Felix is dead, and he went up in smoke along with everyone else we couldn't save." Jude's voice was flat. He was starting to feel detached again, like someone else was saying the words coming out of his mouth. "They did find his suit and helmet. The helmet was broken, and the suit was torn to shreds. I don't need to tell you how impossible that is."

"Yeah, well, a lot of things are impossible," Pixie said. But he didn't seem as optimistic as before, and Jude found some dark pleasure in that. "Until they actually happen. I'm—I'm sorry."

They were both still, heavy silence hanging between them. Then Pixie sighed and held up his hands.

"Okay. I'm gonna level with you. No more tricks, no more word games, no bullshit of any kind, yeah? From now on, we're in this together. You got me. For real."

Jude just stared at him for a couple seconds. In all their interactions before, Pixie had given off the feeling of apprehension, nervous energy, desperately seeking cooperation and approval. There was none of that here. Jude had the feeling that for the first time, Pixie was being entirely honest with him. But none of that actually helped him understand. "Why?"

"I lost someone too," Pixie said with a casual little shrug. He used the same tone as before, when talking about his own death, as if it were simple, obvious, and not overly important. "Sometimes I try to think about what he'd want me to do, and the answer definitely isn't 'mess with you and try to screw you over,' especially when you're kind of in the same boat as me."

"The same boat," Jude repeated, but for once, it wasn't a challenge. He still wasn't sure if he could trust or believe anything Pixie said, but was surprised to notice that he actually wanted to. "Because we both lost someone, and we're trying to put our lives back together?"

"Yeah, pretty much. And neither of us can do it alone."

"I'm not alone," Jude said, defensiveness returning in a heartbeat.

"Your friends aren't really here for you on this, though, are they?" Jude didn't reply. He knew the answer, and knew Pixie knew it, but putting it into words would feel like a betrayal. "That can feel pretty lonely."

Jude stayed quiet for a few seconds, folding his arms across his chest. "They say Felix wouldn't want me to throw away my life, and they're right. I'm lucky to be alive. I shouldn't waste that."

Pixie was quiet for a moment. When he spoke, he didn't meet Jude's eyes, but he didn't sound remotely uncertain either. "I don't think they can really know that for sure, can they? The only one who knows what he'd want is him, and, I mean, sorry for saying this, but Felix isn't around for you to ask anymore. So, sounds to me like you should do your own thing, whatever helps you. Forget what anybody else thinks."

Jude searched Pixie's words for any sign of mockery. He fumbled for an easy, sarcastic response that would re-establish the distance between them. Neither came. "That's... wise."

Pixie grinned, showing his small, pointed canines. "That's punk."

This night, and the one before, had been filled with more strange and ominous changes than Jude could remember experiencing. Not at least for five years. But the most surprising thing yet was how easily he smiled back. "What was their name?"

"Who?" Pixie looked too happy at the reciprocated smile to have quite followed.

"The person you lost."

"Oh." Pixie's own smile didn't so much disappear as slowly evolve into something else, something quiet, reflective, introspective but not shutting down. He wasn't building up walls between them, he was just turning his attention to something buried deep inside them. "Jeff. That was his name. He gave me this."

He held up the guitar, which Jude hadn't taken the time to seriously look at, despite carrying its unwieldy dead weight all the way home. Now, for the first time, he was glad he'd made the effort. Pixie pointed at the sticker, and Jude finally read the phrase he'd only caught in the corner of his eye before: *This Bass Kills Fascists.*

"Huh," Jude said, furrowing his brow. "I don't know much about musical instruments, but I'm fairly certain that's not a bass."

"It's not!" Pixie caught the confusion on his face and chuckled, but in a different way than his usual laugh. He was still turned inward, seeing and remembering things Jude could only guess at.

"See, Jeff got a sticker and put it on his bass, saying, you know, the Woody Guthrie thing, '*This Machine Kills Fascists?*'" Pixie explained. "Except his said '*Guitar*,' like, specifically. And he didn't care, because technically a bass guitar *is* a guitar—but everybody gave him shit for it. Jeff didn't care, he said if people didn't get it, that was their problem. He wouldn't change it. And one day I found a sticker saying the thing, but with 'bass,' and put it on my guitar. A not-bass guitar. Both wrong, both awesome—they match." Now, everything bright and happy did disappear from his face, naturally and all at once, as if it had happened too many times before. "Matched."

"I'm... sorry," Jude said, tentatively and wondering if it was the right thing at all. If there was something else he should say or do. He moved his hand, surprising himself with the automatic impulse to reach out and put it on Pixie's shoulder. But he didn't. Jude might do that with Jasper or Eva—that was why he recognized this, he realized, and felt oddly relieved—but they'd shared five years of tragedy, and many more years of happier history. He'd only known Pixie for two nights, no matter how much familiarity he found. He held still.

"It's fine." Pixie gave a one-shoulder shrug, but didn't meet Jude's eyes. "I'm over it. I mean, as much as possible. I try to focus on the good times, smile because it happened, you know? And think about what he'd say, or want me to do—then do it, that's all. And for real, if Felix was anything like Jeff, he'd tell you not to give up. Not ever. Give the bastards hell."

Jude probably only stared at him for a few seconds, but it felt longer. "Why are you doing this?"

"What?"

"This. Telling me this. Trying to be my friend." He might have said these same words earlier. His voice would have been harder, with a skeptical edge. He would have glared at Pixie instead of looking at him thoughtfully, and wondering what else he'd formed too quick an opinion about.

"Do I need a reason?" Pixie raised his eyebrows and readily met Jude's direct gaze.

"People usually do," Jude said in his same considering tone, evaluating but not rejecting. It was a strange feeling. "Nobody gives you something for nothing, not even if you have things in common."

"That's for sure." Pixie almost smiled again, but his mouth twisted into more of a grimace. "Listen, I shouldn't have tried to play you. I just—I didn't know if I could trust you, so I was trying to get two for the price of one, come out on top with no risk, you know?"

"But you trust me now," Jude said. Again, the words were skeptical, but his tone wasn't.

"More than I did before," Pixie said, nodding. "At first? Nah, why would I? I did the smart thing, seeing how far I could get without giving you a chance to hurt me. But now?" He gave Jude an appraising look as he wiggled a little deeper into the couch cushions, head tilting a little to one side. Jude thought it was a similar expression to the one he wore right now. "You didn't have to save me. You didn't even have to agree to help me in the first place."

Jude shrugged, and broke their shared gaze. Compliments, even indirect ones, always left him unsure what to say. "Anyone else would."

"No, they wouldn't," Pixie said immediately. "They really, really wouldn't. Like you said, nobody gives you something for nothing, and I'm not giving you anything good enough to deserve saving. But you helped me anyway."

"It was nothing." Jude shook his head, but instead of a flare of annoyance, he felt something else. Satisfied? Relieved? Those came close, and neither of them made sense. None of the past two nights had, but the fact that he actually felt... glad about any of it, instead of angry or scared—that made the least sense of all. "Forget it. When we're done, forget it."

"I'm gonna have a hard time doing that." Pixie smiled and, again, Jude couldn't find it in himself to doubt. That was what scared him now, not Pixie. "When I got into this, it was just a deal, yeah. But now it's a promise. This is for real, now. You got me."

Jude didn't know what to say to that, so instead he picked up the half-empty bottle of steak sauce again, and held it out. Pixie accepted and drank the entire thing, looking much more recovered and stable by the time he was done. It was only then that Jude realized he'd been smiling back.

✺ XX JUDGEMENT ✺

ACT FIVE: Descent

"JUST TRY not to do anything... shocking," Jude said, trying to keep the plea out of his voice as he and Pixie approached Jasper's store.

The crowds had thinned out, and they almost had the mall to themselves, a last few underpaid retail workers closing metal shutters across their storefronts and securely locking them. He had no doubt Jasper would be here, though. The few occasions he'd been here after everything else was dark and quiet, he'd noticed Jasper's storefront stayed open, its owner working overtime. Catching up on inventory, he'd said. Jude had honored their unspoken agreement: don't push Jasper for details, and he wouldn't inconveniently remember that Jude didn't actually work nights.

"You got it," Pixie said in a casual tone that did nothing to calm Jude's nerves. But, despite his misgivings, Jude was relieved Pixie was here with him. He'd die before admitting it, but there was just something eerie about a deserted mall. The mannequins in particular.

"I mean it," he said, stopping outside the store entrance. There was one other mall patron left; the woman in black still haunted her regular table, still with her cards and coffee. She raised it to them in a little toast and Jude nodded back, maneuvering Pixie far enough away that their near-whispers wouldn't be overheard. "I've told him as much as he'll let me, so this won't be a complete shock, but there's a difference between knowing and seeing. I don't know if you can ever be ready for it."

"So, showing off the fangs, turning into a bat..." Pixie started to tease, but stopped at the look of increasing apprehension on Jude's face. "Are on the list of things I won't be doing."

"I just don't want to scare him," Jude mumbled, eyes on the doorway he was suddenly having a hard time walking through. Jasper had enough hard days without Jude adding to them.

"So just act natural?" Pixie gave him an unconvincingly wholesome smile. But it was a closed-mouth one, which Jude greatly appreciated under the circumstances.

"Natural is good. Still, maybe it's better if I do the talking, at least to start." Trying to gather his somewhat scattered thoughts, Jude led the way inside, stopping when he saw nobody behind the counter. "Jasper? Are you here?"

"In the back!" Jasper called and, a moment later, the rest of him followed. "Jude! And..." His eyes lit up in recognition, but he was looking past Jude, at the vampire behind him. As he looked at Pixie, his face underwent a strange series of undisguised reactions. First Jasper seemed dumbstruck to see him, then on the edge of panic—but then he seemed to reach some resolution and smiled. It wasn't one of his theatrical grins, it looked a little sad, or maybe resigned. "Pixie. I didn't expect to see you here before sundown."

"I didn't really plan on it either," Pixie said, looking considerably less-chagrined, but still peering at Jude out of the corner of his eye, as if gauging his reaction. Jude didn't have one yet. That required a working brain, and his had just ground to a halt. "But I'm just kind of rolling with it."

"No worries," Pixie said, looking considerably less-chagrined, but still peering at Jude out of the corner of his eye, as if gauging his reaction. Jude didn't have one yet. That required a working brain, and his had just ground to a halt. "Jude had some, so I actually just ate."

"I was wondering when all this would bring us together," Jasper said as he rounded the counter, and Jude stared at them both in increasing bafflement, words failing. "I should have known it'd be sooner rather than later."

"Me too!" Pixie laughed, and it only sounded slightly nervous. "Honestly though, I was gonna drag Jude to you if he didn't think of it himself."

"Wait," Jude said, finding his voice at last and forcing himself back into the present. A present where his oldest friend and newest maybe-friend were already acquainted, and apparently, several steps ahead of him. "Wait. You know each other?"

"We met recently," Jasper said, turning to him, still looking sheepish, and that was strange in itself. Jude couldn't remember him being embarrassed about anything. Jasper refused to be ashamed of his questionable tastes or life decisions, to the extent that Jude thought some of it had to be just to get under his skin—but he looked like he was now. And a little worried. "I was going to tell you, Jude. I just wasn't sure…"

"This is why you weren't surprised," Jude said quietly as comprehension slowly dawned. As he focused his attention on Jasper, Pixie drifted some distance away, wandering through the shelves and surveying their strange contents. He stopped at a silver skull with ruby eyes, looking like he wanted to touch, but deciding against it with a great deal of self-restraint. "When I told you I was working with a vampire the other day. I *knew* something was going on!"

"Yes—and I'm sorry." As he spread his hands, Jasper really looked and sounded it. "Jude, I haven't told you a single untrue thing the entire time we've known one another—but that's not the only way to lie to someone. Lying by omission is still a lie, and it's still a breach of trust, no matter the reason. If that trust is gone, or at least damaged now… I wouldn't blame you."

"Why didn't you tell me?" Jude demanded, still stunned and disoriented by this reversal of circumstances he thought he'd finally gotten a handle on. "All this, just because you didn't want to get involved?"

"I've been involved for a while, I just didn't want to admit it," Jasper said dryly. "But that ship's long since sailed. No, this was about confidentiality," he said with a pointed nod to Pixie, who'd moved on to ogling a glass display case of antique tarot cards. "He came to me for help."

"Jasper probably saved my life," Pixie said, sounding a little more trepidatious and a lot more serious than he usually did. Jasper wasn't the only one to keep a secret from Jude, and Pixie was clearly even less confident in his reaction. "When you asked how I stayed alive? Yeah. You can thank him for me still being around."

"Blood?" Jude managed to ask, still trying to wrap his brain around all this, mentally replaying every conversation he'd had with both of them and scanning for tip-offs. He didn't find any.

"Pretty much the only way," Pixie said with an attempt at a causal shrug, still obviously anxious. "Gotta say, I like the sauce a lot better."

"Sauce?" Jasper asked, sounding intrigued but much calmer than Jude might have been in his place.

"Eva's," Jude supplied, still looking back and forth between them and trying to regain his equilibrium. "Is there a reason you didn't tell me you knew each other?"

"Pixie trusted me not to reveal his existence to anyone who might endanger it," Jasper said, sounding entirely level and reasonable. It didn't make Jude feel better. "And I thought vampire hunters qualified."

Jude glared, feeling unexpectedly defensive. A few nights ago, he would have eagerly agreed with the sentiment. Undead monsters better believe he was a danger to their existences. Now, the idea wasn't nearly as appealing. "You thought I'd try to stake him or something?"

"You did try the holy water," Jasper pointed out, as Pixie scanned a set of leather-bound, parchment-filled books, still not touching but seeming to find them much more interesting than the conspicuously charged conversation going on just a few feet away. "Good thing it didn't work, in retrospect. I'm just as surprised as you are, for the record."

"That was—*he* crashed through *my* window!" Jude struggled to keep his voice down, frustration boiling over. "And you could have still told me you knew each other. It would have been nice to know I wasn't walking into a trap."

Jasper shook his head, seeming to have reached a conclusion he didn't much enjoy. "If I'd told you that, what would you have done?"

"Trusted him a lot sooner," Jude said with growing impatience and indignation. Jasper had always had a much looser definition of rules and the truth than he did, and much of their agreements were unspoken, based on mutual familiarity with trauma, recovery, and things done in the dark no one else would understand. Jude had to chase vampires to function. Jasper had to chase adrenaline in the form of backroom deals of questionable legality. But they'd never actually lied to each other's faces—at least as far as Jude knew. "Is that a bad thing?"

"No. But you had to make that choice on your own, not because of what I wanted."

"You were pretty clear about telling me to go with him!"

"But not because *I* trusted him, that's the difference," Jasper said, every word adamant and emphasized, as if he wanted to will Jude into understanding. "I didn't want you to put my feelings above yours—or trust me more than yourself."

"I do *not*—"

"You just said so, Jude. If I trusted a vampire, that was good enough for you? Enough to make you put aside any of your own feelings, no matter how it hurt? No." He shook his head again while Jude fumed, unsure who he was more upset with, Jasper or himself. "On the other hand, when have you ever listened to sensible advice in general?"

"You still should have told me," Jude said, folding his arms and glowering at Jasper. He didn't like feeling resentful or distrustful of someone who knew him so well, and vice-versa. He didn't like any part of this conversation. "I deserved to know."

"Like I said, we're in different places. I didn't know exactly where you were. And I wasn't going to force you into a recovery you weren't ready for." Jasper was leaning against the counter now, as if he found this interaction exhausting. Jude certainly did, fighting the desire to step around the counter and sink into the chair behind it, as he'd seen Jasper do more and more lately. "Trying to push past these things is never a good idea, ever. Trust me. It would have done so much more harm than good—and not just for you."

"Because I'm damaged," Jude said, voice flat and painfully blunt. "And you thought I'd either kill Pixie, or only trust him because you did."

"Damaged? It takes one to know one," Jasper said with a wan smile. "Grief has a way of muddying the waters. Turning you into someone you don't recognize. But I was wrong, and I misjudged you. Sorely. Jude, I am so, so sorry."

For a few seconds, Jude couldn't answer. He'd started this exchange furious, betrayed. But as the pieces clicked into place, he just felt *tired*. "You were trying to protect us, weren't you? Both of us. Pixie from me, and me from… also me."

"Yes," Jasper said, and Jude could see the hope in his eyes along with the shame. Behind him, Pixie drew a little nearer, perhaps hearing the intensity in their voices die down, or sensing the energetic shift from confrontation to relief. "And I see now, you didn't need it. I should have known better, Jude. I should have trusted you more. Vampire or not, you're not going to go mowing down innocents."

"Innocent?" Pixie actually giggled, though the sound was strained and more than a little awkward after the tense scene that had just played out around him. "Watch it."

"Of course," Jasper said, giving him an answering smile, one with real amusement and fondness, Jude was only slightly surprised to note. He'd only seen Jasper look at him and Eva like that. Maybe he should have been jealous but all he felt, seeing their familiarity, was relief. They clearly got along and that meant less work for him. "Another misjudgment on my part. Deepest apologies."

"For the record, I'm sorry for not saying anything either," Pixie said, still sounding apprehensive despite Jude and Jasper's resolution. "I didn't know if I should. Or if it would change anything. And things were just starting to work out, I didn't want to..."

"Shake anything up, I understand," Jude said, only mildly surprised to find that he actually meant the reassurance. "You played it safe. I might have done the same. In both your places."

"I doubt it," Jasper said with a rueful, but fond, smile. "You've always had a much closer relationship with the truth than I have."

Jude had, in fact, entertained almost that exact thought not long ago, but decided not to share it. "You were doing the best you could, working with bad circumstances," he said instead. "My track record... I might have done something dangerous, yeah. Or at least, you had every reason to think I would, I haven't been the most stable lately. But I don't know what I would have done if I'd ever actually caught a vampire."

"Spray 'em with holy water," Pixie supplied, the smile on his face quickly putting any fears of hard feelings to rest. "Then give them a towel. Listen, you didn't hurt me, which is way more than I expected. All in all, this turned out a lot better than it could've."

"Still," Jude said, still looking at Jasper with a renewed sense of understanding. And, somehow, trust. He wasn't facing all this on his own anymore. Maybe he'd never been. "Last week, if you'd come to me with this... I might have done something I'd regret. But not anymore."

"Really?" Jasper's eyes widened, relief palpable. Relief and something else, what Jude could only think was admiration. "What changed your mind?"

Jude looked over at Pixie, started to answer, then shut his mouth. Pixie made a pleased noise, looking so satisfied Jude almost said something sharp out of habit. But he held his tongue and Pixie's smile grew. "It's good to have friends, isn't it?"

"It is indeed," Jasper agreed, in a tone that suggested this matter was closed, but another was about to open. "And I think I have another one who can help us resolve a potentially treacherous situation, assuming that's why the two of you are here at all."

"Yeah it—wait. Us?" Jude asked, heart fluttering instead of sinking. He was unaccustomed to feeling anything like hope, but he certainly enjoyed it. "You mean you're coming?"

"Of course. The nice thing about the truth being out is that now none of us have to face it alone."

The mall was dark when Jude and Jasper emerged from the shop. Pixie didn't step out with them, instead riding securely in Jude's inside jacket pocket, in his much smaller, winged form. It was safer that way, he and Jasper agreed, and Jude didn't actually mind being the one to give him a ride. There was something oddly comforting about the warm weight in his pocket, and it did more than he would have expected to calm his nerves.

Every other store and kiosk was locked down and deserted, lights turned off, the only illumination from mandatory red EXIT signs and Jasper's store itself. The space seemed much larger, sounds echoing in the stillness. Like the continuous shuffling of cards.

The pale woman in black looked up at Jude and Jasper as they drew near, their reflections clear in the large, black sunglasses Jude had never seen her without, even now. She never once slowed or stopped shuffling, the motion fluid and automatic.

"Sorry to come pester you out of nowhere like this," Jasper began. At the sound of his voice, something started to wiggle in Jude's pocket and Jude tried to angle his body away from the stranger. To his credit, Pixie had been still and quiet for longer than he'd expected, but he'd just have to sit tight a little more. "But it's a bit more urgent than usual."

"You're never a bother," said the woman, shooting him a subtle, crooked smile as she set her deck down and drew one card from the top. She didn't show it to them, but one dark, angular eyebrow rose over her sunglasses. "Whenever I come to see you, I have a good reason and, so far, you've extended me the same courtesy."

"I'd never dream of abusing the privilege," Jasper said and, though his words were unexpectedly formal, it didn't sound like he was faking a bit of sincerity. "We had a request—or maybe an offer. I believe I know your feelings on the subject."

"Sounds intriguing," she said, laying the card down. On it, the moon shone bright silver in a starry night sky. Jude couldn't help feeling uneasy. Jasper, however, looked unbothered. "What kind of request-or-offer?"

"The kind I think we'd all prefer talking about somewhere a bit quieter," Jasper said, with a nod back toward his shop. "I should be closing up soon as well, anyway."

"Hm," she said, turning to face Jude as she lay down a card that looked like a man hanging upside-down from a tree, dangling from a rope around his ankle. "And everyone's up to speed on what deals like mine usually entail?"

"Not as much as I'd like to be," Jude said, shooting Jasper a sidelong glance, not tremendously reassured when he got nothing but a serene smile in return. "Who are you, for starters?"

"A witch," she said, as if it were the most obvious thing in the universe.

"But what's your name?" he persisted.

"Valuable, powerful, and mine to give to those who've earned my trust." She pushed back the floppy brim of her black hat to see them better, reached for her coffee, and took a long sip.

"So we just call you 'Witch,' then?"

"I don't care what you call me. I don't trust you yet." She took another slow drag of coffee and laid a third card. On it, a blindfolded figure in bright yellow was strolling along a forest path, accompanied by a little white dog. She must have seen something in the card she liked, because her half-smile came back and stayed. "But I trust that whatever you're up to with my friend Jasper, it'll be fun."

"Hopefully," Jasper said as she rose, collecting her cards and coffee cup, which unceremoniously disappeared, despite the conspicuous lack of any trash can or bag anywhere around. The cards could have slipped up her sleeve, but the coffee was another story, and Jude felt a small surge of alarm that he quickly controlled, but didn't ignore. "But it could also be quite dangerous."

"My kind of fun, then," she said as Jasper waved them inside and through the dim lighting and packed shelves. They didn't stop at the counter, as Jude expected, instead continuing out through the back exit, into the isolated delivery area that ran behind the mall. The Witch led the way, seeming to already know exactly where she was going. "It's a back-alley kind of night, isn't it?"

"Most are," Jasper returned. He cast an anxious glance toward the alley opening, but the place looked deserted as the mall and he turned back, satisfied. "But tonight more than most. We're going up against someone quite formidable and we'd be exceedingly grateful for any assistance you could provide."

"Who's the formidable someone?" she asked, remarkably casually for all this intrigue. Jude couldn't help but feel a heart-pounding and somewhat nauseating blend of excitement and anxiety. After all this time, he was about to find out what Jasper actually did. And solve the secondary mystery of this ever-present coffee-drinking, card-shuffling enigma.

"A vampire," Jude said abruptly, studying her reaction. He didn't get much of one, just another eyebrow raise from behind her shades. It seemed like she was more surprised by his bluntness than the nature of their request. "He's huge, wears a lot of black leather, and I think he can control other vampires."

"A pair of teenage girls?" she asked without missing a beat. She had an accent he couldn't place. Spanish, maybe, but he didn't think that was quite right.

"That's the one," Jasper jumped in much more cordially, except for shooting Jude a faintly warning look, as if he were starting to make a scene in a fancy restaurant. "I take it you know of him."

"I've dealt with Cruce and his ilk a few times over the years," the Witch said, voice temperature dropping a few degrees as she said his name. "And for years, they've been putting innocent people under their thrall and using them—like those girls. Kids who deserve so much better. The most vulnerable people, these monsters just rake them in and suck the life out of them." Her voice didn't rise, exactly, but it did grow more intense, words coming faster as she spoke. "But they're cowards, like all bullies and tyrants. They resort to mind control to get their way because nobody would give them the time of night otherwise. All those girls need is someone to open their eyes to the truth."

"What truth?" Jude asked, still unsure what to make of the strange woman. For a witch, she'd yet to do anything particularly impressive, aside from making some trash disappear.

"That nobody owns them, fangs or no fangs. They belong to themselves."

"So, what, we just tell them that?" Jude said, skeptical words out of his mouth before he quite decided on them. Still, his first instincts were usually right.

The Witch favored him with a long look that suggested she was keeping her face a practiced neutral in the face of foolish questions. Jude knew the expression, had used it several times to his own advantage, and felt vaguely annoyed at now finding himself on the business end.

"I tell them this *magically,*" she said, in a patient tone that only confirmed Jude's suspicion. "And dispel any holds Cruce has over them, preventing them from being ensnared again. Afterwards, I make sure Cruce never harms them, or anyone else, ever again."

"How?" Jude pressed, feeling himself quickly losing his grasp on the situation and hoping to regain some equilibrium.

The Witch gave a borderline-theatrical shrug, throwing her hands up. "That's entirely up to him—though by now, I have a good idea what he'll choose."

Jude mentally dug in his heels, and physically folded his arms. He was losing ground, he knew, but couldn't bring himself to stop his default, somehow-satisfying stubbornness. At least it made him more sensible. "How do we know anything you're saying is true? How do we know you can help us at all?"

"Ask your friend," she said, nodding to Jasper, who gave her one right back. Jude was also getting tired of the feeling that everybody knew one another, everyone but him. "Better yet, ask your other friend."

"Other...?" he gave her an eyebrow raise of his own, which she didn't acknowledge. Instead, she gave him a faint smirk and deliberate nod.

"The one in your pocket."

Before Jude could respond, the pink bat had wiggled out of his inside jacket pocket and flopped to the pavement. By the time he could look, it had a human shape. Pixie waved in a cheerful way that filled Jude with a sense of foreboding, even as his cheeks flushed with embarrassment. He knew when his bluff had been called—and who'd won this last round.

"How'd you know?" Pixie asked, sounding more tickled than upset that she'd apparently detected his presence. "I mean, yeah, witch, but still."

"I know a lot of things," she said, perfectly nonchalant, as if sensing the presence of bats who turned into punks was nothing unusual. "When vampires are near. Their habits, the way they think. What to do when they become dangers to others, or themselves. How to stay alive while making sure that danger doesn't become a catastrophe."

"Wow," Pixie said, giving her a look of awe which, for some reason, gave Jude a pang of something he refused to name as jealousy. He knew his way around vampires too and he didn't go around bragging about it. But then, even if he tried, the Witch was a lot more convincing than he could ever manage. "Sounds like we're in the right place."

"So you'll do it?" Jasper asked the Witch, sounding more urgent and driven than Jude had heard in a long time. It was refreshing to hear. All this secrecy and danger agreed with him. "You'll help us?"

"Under one condition," she said, and Jude could feel her studying the three of them from behind her dark glasses.

"What's that?" Jude narrowed his eyes, suspicion rising once again.

"I'm going with you."

"Great!" Pixie sounded genuinely excited—even more than usual. "The more the merrier. Jasper already told me how cool you are, so yeah, I think you going with us would be a really smart thing to do." He looked to Jude, noted his dour expression, and continued without a missed beat. "And pissing you off would be really *not*-smart."

"Why?" Jude pointedly refused to meet Pixie's equally pointed look, instead maintaining his stare at the Witch. "What do you really want?"

"Same as you," she said, voice level but with an edge he didn't dare question. "These are dangerous people I've been trying to take down for a very long time. I want them gone, or at least unable to hurt anyone ever again—which, for them, also means 'gone.' This is just the best chance I've had yet."

"So now that's settled," Jasper said with a bright smile and clap. "How exactly do we proceed? I trust you know the way."

"The maintenance tunnels in the sub-basement," she said as if there'd been no interruption. "They open up into a series of tunnels and somewhere in them is your lair."

"Lair?" Pixie repeated, sounding substantially less excited than he had a moment ago. "Why do they have to have a lair? We're vampires, sure, but we don't have to live in creepy tunnels. It's just excessive."

"Maybe," she acknowledged. "But if they're anywhere, they'll be in there. It's dark, hidden, and well-defended. The dramatics don't hurt either. Vampires do tend to enjoy them. Call it a cultural quirk."

"What kind of defenses are we talking about?" Pixie didn't sound at all comforted by her less-than-satisfactory explanation. Jude could relate.

"There's a locked door. You can't get past a lock?" he asked, still eyeing the Witch warily, then glanced over at Pixie. "Or is it like them and needing to be invited or something?"

"That's not the kind of defense I'm talking about," she said with a slight shake of her head, dark brown hair swaying in shoulder-brushing waves. "The place will be magically shielded, fortified. The kind of protection you need me to get you past." Her smirk shifted into something closer to a grimace. "But I've had a lot of time to practice."

"Why haven't you done this before?" Jude had to ask. He was almost hoping to find a hole in their theories, a reason to back out. He'd had reservations about all of this from the beginning and, the more the plan solidified, the more his brain screamed for him to leave, go home, and forget all of this. Except that he'd never be able to forget a single moment.

"Because I'm not a fool," the Witch said easily. "At least not fool enough to risk it on my own. I've met the bastards outside, on my terms, but never theirs. Never on their home territory, and definitely not alone. I don't like the odds. And I don't start fights I'm not guaranteed to win."

"Smart lady." Pixie grinned. He seemed to have taken a real liking to her mysterious vibes and cool confidence. "But the odds are a lot better now that we're here, right?"

"And why exactly is that?" Jude asked, still unconvinced but seeing no alternative. This was happening. Hadn't he always wanted to track down undead evil and drag it to the light? He'd spent years working toward this. Why, then, did he feel so unprepared? "What makes us different from anyone else?"

"He knows his way around the arcane," the Witch said, nodding to Jasper, then Pixie. "And he's an actual vampire. And you... I just have a good feeling about you. You're stubborn, you won't quit for anything, even if it means bashing your head against a brick wall. I like it."

"I'll take that as a compliment, I guess," Jude said with grudging satisfaction.

"Takes one to know one," she tossed back. "So, there we are. You get me there, I'll get you in, we'll get each other out alive—or close enough."

"Deal?" Jude asked, hoping he wasn't making a huge mistake. At least if he was, he told himself, he wouldn't be alone.

The witch gave that same tight-lipped smile that made him shiver and wonder what in the world came next. "Deal."

"Do you trust her?" Jude asked as he followed Jasper down the length of the loading alley, toward the open street. The Witch did not accompany them. Jude had turned his back for what must have only been a second but, when he looked back, she'd disappeared as if she were never there. He wasn't actually surprised by this, considering the rest of the past few days—and his life in general—but it was still mildly unsettling.

"As much as I trust anyone who isn't you or Eva," Jasper said, casually, as if they were discussing dinner plans with a new acquaintance.

"So then, not much?" Jude couldn't resist a slight smirk, the kind she had seemed so fond of. It was easier to feel optimistic when they had a plan, or at least less-than-doomed. They may still be lost causes, but Jude was starting to warm to the challenge. However this night turned out, he'd be closer to answers, closure, and sweet resolution than he'd ever come.

"Not as much as I'd like to," Jasper said a bit more seriously. "But don't worry. She'll help us."

"That's not all I'm worried about..." Jude felt something move in his pocket. Pixie was in there, again, and Jude unconsciously gave the warm lump a quick, reassuring pet.

Jasper gave a soft chuckle and started to answer, probably to say something ironic-but-comforting in the way only he could accomplish, the way Jude loved—but stopped mid-word. Then he stopped walking and held perfectly still.

"Jasper?" Jude asked, alarmed, and turned around.

But he didn't reply. His eyes were wide and frightened, staring at—no, past Jude. At something behind and above him. Slowly, hating every moment, Jude turned again. He knew what it would be, but he made himself look anyway. And, as his eyes fell on the monster, he made himself breathe.

The shadowed figure clinging to the sheer brick wall twenty feet in the air was a vampire. Jude didn't need to see its fangs to know that, but they were bared, flashing white and long as his pinkie finger, sharper than any he'd ever seen. The form was unmistakably inhuman, viscerally alien, and Jude knew the horror and revulsion he felt seeing its elongated limbs and claws was evolutionary, as millennia-ingrained as a fear of heights, fire, or death. This kind of fear kept humans alive. Except for when there was no escape.

The creature dropped silently, seeming to rush forward before it even hit the ground. Jude raised his fists but the action was absurd, pointless. The thing was a blur. He had a better chance of catching the wind itself in his hand than landing a punch, but he had to do something, anything. If they were going down, he was going down swinging.

But mid-dash, the vampire stopped, seeming every bit as frozen as the terrified pair of humans before it. And, for one brief, terrible moment, its outlines became clear, illuminated by one of the few alley street lights.

In a heartbeat that seemed to stretch into years, into a lifetime, Jude saw the creature's face. Like the others he'd seen, it was twisted into a monstrous grimace. But as he watched, blood freezing in his veins, the horrific snarl faded, and the warped lines and too-sharp angles of the creature's chillingly morphed features smoothed until they resolved into something else. Something Jude knew. As he stared into the vampire's partially-transformed face, a pair of very human, very familiar eyes stared back.

He knew that face. Jude was sure he'd know the voice within a single word. He'd know it anywhere: dreaming and devastated, awake and unafraid, asleep or dead.

Everything had changed the day Felix died. Except for his eyes.

But the moment Jude barely began to articulate this, that those were the eyes that he hadn't seen for five years, except for dreams from which he awoke screaming, crying, he hadn't expected to see them ever again, even looking at pictures was beyond him, and now here they were, *here he was*—

He was gone.

In another rush of wind and blurred, too-fast-to-track movement, Felix was gone. Again.

Jude couldn't move. Beside him, Jasper stood frozen as well, staring into the darkness where the... where Felix had disappeared. Something wiggled in Jude's pocket, and he automatically reached down to cover the pink, fuzzy head that poked out. Pixie had to be scared, or at the very least curious, but Jude couldn't make his mouth work. He couldn't make any part of himself move.

"Jude," Jasper whispered, breaking the horrified silence. "Did you see—"

The impact to his chest was so fast Jude never saw it coming, and so forceful he staggered backwards until he hit the brick wall. Jude gasped, the wind knocked out of him and head spinning as the impossibly fast-moving creature flashed before him again. Before he could catch his breath, or make a sound, it was directly in front of him, claws reaching for him, grabbing at his jacket. Then, a high-pitched screech and rapid flapping sent a new kind of dread surging through him.

"No!" Jude shouted, forcing his eyes open and hands into fists as talon-like claws tore at his jacket and its inner pocket, then seized the small, pink, frantically flapping bat. "No, don't touch him! Get—"

Felix's hands. Gentle, healing, magic hands. Shoving Jude against the wall and crushing Pixie in their grip, in their *claws.* Jude felt like he was dying, he couldn't breathe, he wanted to vomit and scream and drag the thing with Felix's face into the light, look it in the horrifically familiar eyes until he saw the truth, dredge some kind of meaning from this nightmare—

Felix recoiled, springing back and up into the air, Pixie clutched tight in both hands. There was another flapping sound, much louder than Pixie's desperate flailing, and a pair of huge, dark wings unfurled from his back. They nearly spanned the alley and a gust of wind hit Jude in the face. More flaps, more wind-bursts, and more of Pixie's terrified squeaks—and Felix leaped into the air, powerful clawed legs and wings propelling them higher and faster than anything should be able to move, almost faster than the human eye could follow.

Then they were gone.

Jude almost collapsed, laid low by terror, panic, and shame. He almost froze, overwhelmed with terror and shock. He almost ran after them, screaming Felix's name, and Pixie's. He almost laughed hysterically, weak under the realization that he'd been right, that what he'd barely dared hope for five years was real, that *he knew what he'd seen.*

"Jasper!" he yelled the second he got his breath back. Instead of any of the above tempting choices, Jude shoved his horror aside, banished the memory of Felix's face and hands forever burned into his brain, a precious memory now tainted by fangs and claws. If he let himself, Jude knew he'd sink into a well of despair from which he might never emerge, and now that simply was not an option. "Damn it, come on! They're getting away! Fuck that, they're already gone! They're gone, and he took Pixie, and *we have to go after them! Now!"*

Jasper didn't move. He hadn't moved this entire time.

"Come on, move! Say something!" Jude barely resisted reaching out and shaking him. He could feel his own desperation rising. A panic attack was the absolute last thing he needed right now, but it was the absolute most likely thing if this kept getting worse, and especially if Jasper wouldn't talk to him. "Anything!"

"You saw who that was." Jasper's voice was barely audible, but it wasn't a question. When Jasper turned to face him, he looked almost as grey as any vampire Jude had seen.

"Yes," he made himself answer, though the words tasted like blood on his tongue. "Felix. He's…"

"He's alive." Jasper finished when Jude couldn't. His voice did not shake, and grew stronger with every word. There was no hesitation, only certainty, finality. "He's *been* alive all this time."

It wasn't quite true, Jude thought with a surge of hysteria. But it didn't have to be completely true to be forever life-changing. Felix wasn't alive, but he wasn't dead. He wasn't gone, he was here. *He'd been here. He was just—*

Jude sucked in a breath. His chest was tight, the familiar constriction that meant he was right on the panic-edge again. This was real. As he'd said over and over again for years, Jude knew what he saw. And he'd seen *Felix*.

But that wasn't the only thought that made his stomach drop. Felix was here. And Pixie wasn't. Pulling himself together as much as humanly possible when dealing with new, inhuman realities, Jude made himself speak. "So, assuming that was—who we thought it was—"

"It was!" Jasper said immediately, starting to pace quickly back and forth, eyes bright. Even through his dissociative fog, Jude realized Jasper sounded more energetic, more *alive* than he could remember hearing, even after tonight's excitement leading until this moment. "It *is!* I'd know him anywhere! At the end of the world! Fangs be damned, that was him!"

"Okay. Okay," Jude said, still trying to get his breathing and pounding heart under control, and arrange his chaotic thoughts into anything resembling sense. "So he... flew at us. He attacked us. And he took Pixie."

"Yes," Jasper said, stopping his pacing and looking at Jude. The intensity in his eyes was startling, as if he'd been asleep for the past five years and only just now awakened. "Yes, he—but he wasn't in his right mind. How could he be? *I* haven't been in my right mind, none of us have."

"A thrall," Jude said, throat feeling thick as he remembered Pixie's ominous words and the Witch's confirmation. He started to shake. "He's under Cruce's control just like the girls. He has to be. Nothing else makes sense."

"My God," Jasper whispered. "My God, all this time, I can't imagine..."

With that, all the galvanized energy in Jasper's eyes, voice, and body seemed to dissipate, like a candle blown out by a gust of cold wind. Slowly, he sank down to sit on the curb, burying his face in his hands in a now-familiar position that made Jude's heart ache.

"If Felix is a vampire and he took Pixie," Jude started, frantically clinging to logical thought-processes, cause and effect, his best shot at making sense of this nightmare. Where would they be? Where were they headed right now? He had an idea, and didn't like it one bit. "That means he's—"

"Jude," Jasper said, very quietly, without looking up. His shoulders sagged and Jude felt his own knees shake with shock and exhaustion. "Give me a moment to take this in. Please?"

Jude stood in silence for the space of a few long breaths. Then, just as silently, he sat down on the curb beside Jasper and let his own head drop onto his knees. They'd figure out the next step soon. But for right now he just had to sit.

Felix was here. Pixie was gone. And Jude was numb.

"The sub-basement, she said!" Jasper exclaimed with a sudden urgency, raising his head. His revitalized voice shook Jude back to the present before he could sink too far into despair. That, at least, was familiar. "That's where they will have gone! It all comes back to the same place!"

"That's what I was thinking." At least while he was able to think at all. But now Jude shook his head to clear the shock-induced cobwebs. Action. Game plan. They needed one. Jasper was with him, at least. "It makes sense."

"You have the key, correct?" Jasper prodded. The hope in his voice made Jude's heart speed up, made his head spin with something aside from overwhelmed confusion.

"No, not me," Jude said, grounding himself with the feel of the cold concrete on which he sat, digging his fingertips into the curb. "Eva."

"Shit." Jasper sighed, sounding much more tired than annoyed. "I tried to tell her too, you know? But she didn't want to hear it, and some things shouldn't be forced. But she needs to know, should have known for a long time. How are we going to explain this?"

"Let me worry about that," Jude reassured him, speaking as if he had a plan and wishing he knew what it was. "Go back and talk to your friend the Witch, get everything ready. I'll meet you at the entrance with the key."

"All right," Jasper nodded quickly, climbing to his feet but not moving away just yet. He extended a hand down to Jude, which was gratefully taken. "This is happening. It's a nightmare, but it's real, and we know what to do with that. Save the shock and breakdowns for later. We've both gotten quite good at compartmentalizing, haven't we? So we keep moving for just a little longer and we'll know the truth. Just a bit more and he'll be…"

He trailed off, eyes slipping out of focus, and Jude found himself smiling through the pain. Jasper never was the best at taking his own advice.

"I don't know how this ends," Jude told him, not letting go of his hand, taking some small solace in the warmth and closeness. They'd been together all through these long, painful years, but the kind of togetherness that reminded him of being in the same empty house, in different rooms. Tonight they were in the same place. "But it's been a long time coming. Five years too long."

"Jude, I'm sorry about Pixie," Jasper said after a short pause. He shut his eyes briefly, and when he opened them again they were clear and resolved. Compartmentalization was a hell of a thing, Jude thought. "We'll get him back too, I pr—"

"It's fine," Jude said before Jasper could finish that wonderful, dangerous word. He knew firsthand how much it hurt to make promises he couldn't keep. The possibility that this might be one of them made his heart clench all over again.

"None of this is fine," Jasper said with a sad return smile that Jude knew much more intimately than any of his newly-reclaimed, brave, wild hope. "It hasn't been fine for a long time. And we're right on the edge of it, now, aren't we? It might be all over tonight… or, dare to dream, we might have everything."

Jude nodded, giving the warm fingers in his hand a squeeze. His eyes stung, like looking into the smoke and flames of an inferno. But at least, just like before, he wouldn't walk into it alone.

"Thank you," he said softly, a familiar ache flaring in his chest. He'd felt it before, but never expected to find himself aching for the safety and return of someone who'd come into his life through noise complaints and a broken window. None of it had prepared him at all. "I… Pixie's just… it wouldn't be fair not to hold up my end of our deal. Not after all this."

"I know," Jasper said just as quietly, with just as much certainty. He let go and stepped away, heading back the way they'd come. "And you're welcome."

"I need help," Jude said the moment the door opened.

"I've been saying," was Eva's deadpan reply. The sun had just gone down and she was in red flannel pajama bottoms and an oversized red T-shirt reading *Meet Me In The Pit*. Probably just settling in for a relaxing evening of Netflix and alcohol that she so sorely needed and deserved, Jude thought with a pang.

"No, I mean, I need *your* help," he clarified, fighting the urge to clench his teeth and hyperventilate. No good would come from breaking down, particularly not now. But it sure was tempting. "I need to get into the maintenance tunnels. The mall's sub-basement. It's important."

"Now?" Eva raised her eyebrows and leaned against the doorframe. At any other time, Jude might have taken the hint.

"Yes. Right now."

"At night." She glanced down at her pajama bottoms and bare feet, then back up at him, looking caught between fatigue, annoyance, and concern.

"Yes!" Jude said, as firmly but calmly as he could manage. "Tomorrow will be too late."

"Because…?"

He knew the apprehensive look on Eva's face. It meant she was praying to every guardian angel who might be listening that he wasn't about to spout anything about blood and fangs. Jude had seen that pleading look a lot. Most recently just a few days ago, when he'd stood in her office and tried to fill out an incident report involving undead skaters. Now the situation was so much more important, so much more deadly, and he couldn't begin to explain why. "I can't tell you."

Her shoulders sagged as she sighed, staring at him with half-mast eyes. "Jude… I'm tired."

"I know," he said, heart sinking. He felt every bit as worn out as she did, had for five years. The only difference between them was how they responded. "And you have every right to be, and I'm sorry I keep doing this to you. I wouldn't if I could possibly avoid it, please believe me. I'm trying. It's about…"

"About what, Jude?" Eva prompted, pinching the bridge of her nose. It still looked like it hurt.

"It's about someone important to me."

After the words were out, Jude was only mildly surprised to find they were absolutely true. And that he didn't just mean the shocking revelation about Felix—though the horrible knowledge was so momentous he could barely think about it without collapsing. He didn't know exactly when his dynamic with Pixie had shifted from reluctant partnership to… something else. But it had. And the thought of him alone and surrounded by hostile vampires made Jude's stomach drop nearly as much as it did when he thought about the alien look in Felix's eyes.

"Tell me what's going on," she said, taking a step back, away from the door, and nodding for him to follow. She was going to hear him out, just like he'd prayed. Not known, not counted on, or taken for granted. Eva would have been so very justified to blow him off after this. But she was listening. It was all he could ask. "The truth, Jude. No vampires. No full moon. Just… the truth."

"My missing upstairs neighbor, Pixie," Jude started as he followed her inside, slowly, measuring his words. There had to be a way to distill the truth, tell her the crux of his crisis without getting into dangerous territory. "He's not so missing anymore."

"Well, that's good," Eva said, blinking and looking a little nonplussed at the anxiety on her friend's face. Clearly she'd expected a different direction. Jude took this as encouragement and continued. "Glad to hear he's okay."

"Yeah. And he was helping me deal with some… troublemakers," he said, unable to help raising his eyebrows meaningfully. "Kids at first, but then a bigger, meaner one appeared last night—but then he…"

Felix. Jude couldn't possibly tell her yet. It was too much to process, too much for him to even make sense of yet. It was almost more painful to think about Felix now, knowing in what form he'd survived. How much he had to have suffered for five long years. There had been nights where Jude thought Felix had been the lucky one. But Felix had received no merciful release of death, no cessation of pain—instead granted what appeared to be a half-living servitude. This was almost worse. He didn't know. He couldn't know until this was over.

"Someone took him," Jude finished a little weakly. He was suddenly so, so tired.

"To the maintenance tunnels?" Eva said, studying him, as if carefully searching for a lie in anything Jude had said. She wouldn't find one. But she knew she wasn't getting the whole truth either, Jude could tell that just by looking. They never could keep things from one another, even the most painful or unbelievable. As Jasper had recently observed, there was more than one way to tell a lie to someone, ways that involved no words at all. None of that had a place here.

"That's where Jasper thinks they went," Jude said with a nod. "The—the bad people, that's where they've got Pixie. So we have to hurry and get down there too."

Eva brought one fist up to her face, tapping it gently against her mouth and nose, elbow propped up with her other hand. She let out a long sigh through her nostrils, looking at Jude as if he were a puzzle she'd been so close to solving, but suddenly discovered a new, ill-fitting piece. "Jasper's going and I'm not?"

So close. Their next few words would determine so much more than one night. It felt like a friendship and hard-won trust hung in the balance right along with Pixie. Jude took in a slow, deep breath, and let it out. "I want to know you're safe."

"That's a cop-out and you know it," Eva said, eyes narrowing. He'd known it was the wrong answer when he said it, but didn't have anything better to offer. "If you're going somewhere really dangerous—which I'd say you are—you need me."

"I need someone on the outside to call for help if I don't come back," he said, a shake in his voice he refused to acknowledge. "Two in, two out, remember?"

"By my count, there's two in, one out." Was it his imagination, or did the specter, the ghost of a smile flit across her face when he reminded her of the old firefighting maxim? Always work in pairs. Never leave your partner. Two go into an active building and two come out. Her smile was gone before it really materialized, and only her careful, searching stare remained.

"And thank God for that one," he said, meaning every word. That old rule had another meaning—two venturing inside, two staying outside, in constant radio contact and ready for damage control. That was the one he needed her to remember. "Eva, I trust you more than anybody else on the planet. I *want* you to come with us. I *want* to show you everything. But it's not about that anymore, it's about staying alive and the only way I see us coming out of this is if you're out here keeping an eye on everything before it goes to hell. Just like how it used to be. I could run into anything if I knew you were watching up above me."

"But I'm not," she said, and now he could hear the anxiety in her voice. But it wasn't rejection. It wasn't dismissal. It was the fear that came from being in the trenches right beside someone, the deep breath before you both took the plunge. "You're not going to have cell reception down there. You'll have no way to call for help."

"I know. It would be too late anyway," Jude spoke quietly, words coming out faster now. "But I'll call you as soon as we're out. I promise. If I don't— Eva, I've broken a lot of promises lately. But if I break this one, if the sun comes up and you haven't heard from me? You'll know it's real, and it's over, and we need that extraction..." *if there's anything left to extract,* went his unspoken conclusion. He had no doubt that she'd understand that much at least. "So just... please," he said, looking directly into her eyes with a fervor he hadn't felt in years. He recognized the energy flowing through him now, the conviction, the desperate hope. He'd seen it in Jasper's eyes not long ago. "Give me one last chance. When I'm done, I'll either show you everything, or I'll be dead. Either way, it'll be over."

Eva didn't answer right away. For a few second she held absolutely still and then, slowly, sank down onto her own living room sofa—black leather and a lot less ragged than Jude's. She sat there, staring at the opposite wall, while Jude stood there and silently waited, hating the infusion of tension and unaccustomed awkwardness between them. Eva was quiet for a long time.

"When the sun comes up?" she asked at last, very softly, and Jude knew, *knew* with his entire heart, what she was really asking. In a way not entirely unlike Jasper knowing Felix's face at the end of all things, Jude knew Eva's voice. He knew the exhaustion, the *just-one-more-step* resolve, the wanting to believe, but being unable to muster the hope.

He also knew he would never be able to lie to her. Not when she asked him in that voice. Not ever. Jude shut his eyes and readied himself for the end. "Yes."

Silence stretched between them. The silence he'd been waiting for, for years. She'd been entirely within her rights to cut him off, him and all his ridiculous vampire bullshit. They had very different coping methods, as she'd say. Jude obsessed and clung to evanescent ghosts and ran full-tilt through the very fire that burned him. Eva did her best to move on and hold herself—and them—together. Do her job. Make life better for the people left.

He had no right to ask this of her. She deserved to heal on her own, away from all of this. Away from him. If that was what it took, he wished her resolution, closure, and peace with all his cracked and fire-tarnished heart.

The words that finally broke the silence weren't the ones he expected to hear. But they were also the impossible culmination of the wild, foolish hope he didn't know he'd been praying for, even as he knew exactly how impossible, how unfair it all was.

"I'll help," Eva said softly and Jude felt his painstakingly-built defenses crumble in the most beautiful way. "Do what you need to do. I've got your back."

Tears stung at his eyes and he gasped out a sob. It was never the panic in the midst of a crisis that got him, it was the relief after. Kindness, not pain. That he was never prepared for.

"Thank you," Jude whispered, squeezing his eyes shut. The tears came anyway but, right now, with her, he didn't care. He never did. "I... thank you. So much. I can't even say how much this means."

"I think I have a pretty good idea," Eva said, and Jude didn't need to open his eyes to hear the smile in her voice. The last thing he expected or deserved. But coming from her, it felt natural. Right. Being together always did. "But this is the last time. I've been saying that too."

"I know," Jude said, opening his swimming eyes and blinking her back into focus.

"And this time I mean it." The finality in her voice and face was unmistakable. After five years of promises desperately made and hopelessly broken, neither one of them had the energy required. "Don't make me regret it, Jude. Please. Make it worth it."

"It's worth it. I promise, it is." He dragged a forearm across his eyes, rubbing so hard it hurt. "You didn't have to say yes. It's not fair to ask you anything, after all the shit I've pulled. I know that."

"Yeah, I know it too," Eva sighed, and they both had to smile just a little.

"So then why are you doing this?" Jude never knew how to handle the non-worst scenario. Even now, with a found and hard-kept sister he trusted so much more than his own fool self. No trust could keep him from questioning.

She pulled him into a hug so tight he couldn't breathe. He sobbed again, forehead against her shoulder, and hugged her back like both of their lives depended on it. "Because it's about someone important to me."

"*Pixie*. What am I going to do with you?" Cruce's grating voice was conversational. The rebuke was almost fond, a soft disapproval, like one might show a pet who'd made a mess on a fancy rug. Pixie felt sick.

He also couldn't move. Restrained, he thought. Somehow. Pixie hung in the nebulous state between unconsciousness and waking, head heavy, eyes throbbing, limbs feeling like lead. But that meant he had human arms and legs.

Pixie remembered snuggling down into the cozy warmth of Jude's pocket. Then, yelling. Fear in Jude's voice. Poking his head out and smelling more fear on the breeze, along with another, familiar, inhuman scent. Then being seized in a tight grip, desperately flapping to get away before being restrained, rushing through the air, a crushing impact, pain—

Then, nothing.

"I'd say I didn't want to do this, that you pushed me here, but that would be a lie," Cruce's voice continued, unwaveringly light and casual. "And I do try to avoid direct lies. Particularly when the truth is so much fun. I've been looking forward to every minute of this."

He moved away then, and Pixie heard more than saw him pick something up. Instinct flooded back along with barely-restrained panic from fragmented memories; *Cruce enjoyed working in the dark*. Fortunately, Pixie's strongest sense was no longer sight. He'd never known if that was an advantage, or if Cruce used that sensitive hearing against him. Hearing without seeing and never being able to stop whatever came could be even more terrifying…

"I will say, however," Cruce said with a sigh, as if ruminating over tragic regrets. It sounded like he was behind Pixie now, and the realization sent a wave of fear crashing through Pixie's entire body. He wanted to curl up into a ball. He wanted to turn back into a bat and fly away. He couldn't do either. Couldn't even move. Even if he could, he knew what would happen if he did. "Part of that *is* true. This *is* all your doing. You knew what would happen the moment you ran. And you did it anyway! I wasn't the only one disappointed, let me assure you."

Cruce gave a rueful click of his tongue from somewhere Pixie couldn't see. Pixie shivered.

"And now, you've put me in a very uncomfortable dilemma," Cruce continued, voice low and smooth. He ran one finger down Pixie's neck, drawing a frightened gasp and shiver, and tugged lazily at his scarf. Pixie clamped his mouth shut, barely suppressing the whimper that badly wanted to escape—but couldn't keep in the relieved sigh when Cruce's claw released his scarf and moved away from his neck.

"You see, no matter how glad I am to see you again, and particularly under these circumstances," Cruce continued, sounding an odd combination of smug and vaguely annoyed. "Our master was *very* clear about the condition in which I'm to see you returned. That being 'good as new, no marks, no damage.' But, I'm afraid, sometimes things just don't work out as we planned."

Pixie gasped as something painful pressed into the palm of his left hand. A sharp object with a terrible point, but he couldn't identify exactly what. Cruce was still behind him, stretching his arm to an awkward, uncomfortable angle. He let out a faint whimper, but immediately clamped his mouth shut over it. He knew from experience that Cruce didn't just feed on blood. He liked the fear that preceded it, too.

"For example, I wasn't supposed to leave scars. But sometimes exceptions have to be made." He could hear the cruel smile in Cruce's voice. Could tell that he'd heard Pixie's soft, fear-filled sound. Of course he had. "And after all, you weren't supposed to run away in the first place. I'd call that even."

The sharp pain in the middle of his palm intensified. But, strangely, it didn't feel like Cruce was digging it in. The point in his palm burned, as if it were metal, superheated. Pixie could almost smell his own scorched flesh. Only one thing could burn his skin like that now, he thought, despairingly.

Cruce moved into his field of vision now. His smile was every bit as wicked as Pixie had imagined. And the hammer he raised over his head shone as brilliantly silver as the nail he held against Pixie's hand.

"Keep your eyes open," he whispered, making Pixie's stomach twist in agonized, nauseating terror. "And keep quiet. It'll all go easier if you do."

The hammer fell, and Pixie disobeyed one more time.

Eva's key was as good as her word and that, as always, was very good. The door to the maintenance tunnels opened at the turn of the key. Jude and Jasper followed the Witch's lead as she stepped over the threshold, leaving the mall, and the rest of the world, behind them.

Jude had made a brief stop at his own apartment before joining them, looking for anything he could use for what promised to be a harrowing night. The first thing he found was the empty bottle that had once held the alleged holy water, which seemed no more effective against vampires than regular water. An empty bottle was even more useless. For the first time, Jude wished he'd actually invested in the archetypal anti-vampire weapon, a stake. He'd never bothered to obtain one. Somehow having a real weapon would have made everything even more real and terrifying—but he didn't have time to examine his motivations, and instead grabbed the only item that might actually be helpful. Another bottle. Red, long-necked, and filled with sauce instead of holy water.

Now, as he headed down the corridor with Jasper and the Witch, he kept touching the cool weight in his inside jacket pocket, somehow reassured by its presence as they went. The walls and ceiling gradually changed from the uniform lines and angles of constructed concrete to rough stone. Bare-bulb lights hung from the ceiling, just a bit too far apart for comfort, casting strange shadows as the rock surface grew irregular. The corridor's shape grew more organic, until they were walking down a round-walled tunnel that sloped continually down.

After around ten minutes, they reached another door set into the stone. It looked just like the heavy metal door to the mall's sub-basement they'd passed through, but something about it felt... wrong. Jude stopped several yards away from it, heart speeding up.

Going through that door was a bad idea, he just knew. The very thought made cold terror rise through his chest, freezing around his heart and lungs. Behind him, Jasper stopped as well, making no attempt to pass Jude or keep walking—the Witch, however, didn't break stride.

As she continued toward the door without hesitation, she raised her hands, then made a sweeping motion as if pushing something aside, or opening invisible curtains. With two more unerring steps, she reached the door and took hold of the handle with both hands, pulling it open with only a soft sound of exertion. When she was done, she stood to one side and gave a slight bow, gesturing grandly to it with both hands.

"So that's my end of the bargain held up," the Witch said, sounding satisfied with her part in the operation. "Or the first step, anyway. Feel better?"

Jude gave a shaky nod, breathing more easily. The moment she'd opened the door, the dread that had once built up in his chest was gone. It felt like that door had been radioactive, giving off every possible danger sign, intangible but impossible to ignore until she'd found the magical 'off' switch. Beyond the open door, the corridor continued.

"Thank you," Jasper said, sounding as disoriented as Jude felt. He looked from the Witch to Jude, then back at the door, seeming to struggle with something internally. "Ah, did either of you happen to feel...?"

"I definitely did," Jude confirmed, remembering the *negativity* radiating off that door with a chill. At least it was over now. There seemed to have been an atmospheric shift, and everything felt a lot lighter, as if the air were pressurized instead of high-altitude thin. "It didn't feel like a good sign."

"It wasn't a bad one, either," said the Witch, sounding enviably unbothered. "Expect some more strangeness as we go, but nothing we can't handle."

Jude gritted his teeth, kept his reservations to himself, and followed.

Even with the door's unnatural sense of dread dissipated, his sense of foreboding grew with every passing moment. Jude couldn't help feeling like they were venturing someplace humans weren't supposed to be, or even know about, and every step brought them further from daylight and fresh air and closer to a death trap from which there could be no escape.

But he kept walking and said nothing. Nobody did, not as the corridor branched, then branched again, dark paths leading away. Not as the Witch led them deeper into the earth, taking some turnoffs and passing others without hesitation. Nobody questioned her or how she knew where they were going at all—not until the dark, claustrophobic tunnel network opened up.

At first, Jude thought they were outside. Where the tunnel's air had been cool but increasingly stale, the breeze that met his skin smelled fresh. The sounds of their footsteps and shallow breathing didn't echo in the same way as they had in the tunnel's small space. They'd entered a much larger cavern and, as his eyes adjusted gradually, he saw that it wasn't as pitch-dark as he'd thought, but illuminated by a low, intangible light, the source of which he couldn't find.

"What is this place?" he asked, voice reverberating through the deep, open space. "I've never heard of a cave this size around here. Or any at all, actually."

"You weren't supposed to," the Witch answered. She still sounded considerably less awed and more casual, as if huge, previously-unknown caves were a normal part of her everyday life.

"Look, there's more tunnels over there," Jasper observed, sounding incredulous and admiring at the same time. "If there's even one more cave like this one, this network must stretch under the entire city…"

Jude could see him point in the low light and followed the outline of his finger to what had to be the far end of the cave. At least one hundred feet across the dark, open space were even darker shapes—dozens of entrances to more tunnels like the one through which they'd come. The light was stronger on the cavern's far side, increasing until it looked like dim twilight underground.

"How has nobody ever noticed?" he marveled, brain failing to reconcile any of this. Like so many things in his life, it didn't make sense. At least not when viewed through a lens that expected anything like rationality.

"Pocket dimension," said the Witch, as if that explained everything.

"Pocket...?" Jude repeated, uncomprehending.

"A slice of reality solely dedicated to a single place or time. It's practical, economical," she said with a shrug. "Not really that unusual. It saves space. And nobody gets to see that space unless they're allowed, or good enough to bypass its tricks."

"We're in... another dimension right now?" Jude whispered, suddenly feeling a little dizzy. His brain was going to reach its limit soon, he knew.

The Witch's smirk was faint in the dim light, but unmistakable. "As I said, nothing we can't handle."

Before anyone could answer, everything changed. Light exploded through the cavern, drawing a surprised gasp from Jude as he squeezed his eyes shut and stumbled back, running into somebody, he couldn't tell who, couldn't tell where the light had come from—but he knew what it meant. They were no longer alone.

"Ah, wonderful! You took the bait," called a clipped male voice, followed by a clap that snapped through the calm cavern air. "And here you are!"

"Yes," came the Witch's voice, calm, with an edge of fury instead of mockery. "Here we are. And you know what comes next. You can avoid some of it if you let him go."

Let him... Jude forced his eyes open, terrified of what he'd see, but even more terrified to keep them closed.

Cruce. The towering vampire wore the same black leather as before, the same gloves. He stood not far away from the three, much closer than he should have been given there had been no audible approach. On either side of him, torches blazed in wall sconces, casting the blinding light. They were too bright to look at without pain and Cruce stood in the glaring spot between them. Now his and every other shadow in the cavern danced unnervingly in the too intense firelight.

But none of that mattered. Pixie was here, Jude thought as he rubbed at his sore eyes, trying desperately to blink the purple-and-orange afterimages away. He had to be.

When he finally found Pixie, slightly off to one side and outside Cruce's immediate spotlight, Jude wished he hadn't.

Pixie was back in human form and Jude had to look up to see him. Strangely, he was positioned above the much-larger Cruce. Hanging from something. Dangling. His arms were spread wide, but the droop of his head—and his silence—told Jude he was unconscious. Perhaps mercifully, Jude thought, sickened. He couldn't quite tell what Cruce had done to Pixie and perhaps that was merciful too. Jude's mind refused to put the pieces together. All that mattered was that Pixie was *here*. Not unharmed, but alive.

Despite everything, Jude still had no real idea what could actually harm or kill a vampire. Apparently not fire, he'd had five years to wrestle with that. Not holy water, as he'd found out firsthand. Then what—

"You haven't changed." The Witch's voice was harder than before, and actively aggressive for the first time. Jude shivered, but couldn't be sure if it was fear of her rage, or revulsion at—at whatever Cruce had done to Pixie. He couldn't stop staring, but still couldn't identify what was happening. What was wrong.

"Why tamper with perfection?" Cruce shot back, an unpleasant laugh under his echoing words. He bared his teeth in a grin as he looked up at Pixie's still form. "Especially when it's something I just… thoroughly enjoy. That's rare, nowadays—we have to take pleasure where we can. And inspiration, though I'm admittedly not sure if this qualifies as 'divine.'"

Divine inspiration.

No.

In a flash, Jude understood what his weary and traumatized brain was trying to protect him from. The way Pixie's arms were outstretched, the way his head hung down low. The angular shape behind him. The glints of metal in his palms. He'd seen this before. He hadn't seen it for five years but, before that, he'd seen it every Sunday.

"Oh, God," Jude whispered, voice too loud for the silence, heartbeat too loud in his ears. Bile rose in his throat, burning all the way up, and his stomach constricted. He wanted to follow the impulse, vomit right on the spot, but that would mean looking away, and he couldn't look away any more than he could breathe—and the moment he'd laid eyes on Pixie, he'd forgotten how.

"Crude, perhaps," Cruce said, cruel amusement raising every hair on the back of Jude's neck. "But it gets the job done. A time-honored punishment for thieves."

His scarf, Jude realized, dizzied brain latching onto a single, small, but oddly important detail. Pixie wasn't wearing it anymore. Jude had never seen him without it before, but here…

"Thieves…?" Jude rasped, head spinning. This wasn't happening. This couldn't be real. "What—"

"Did he steal?" Cruce interrupted, raising one hand to cup his ear. The exaggerated motion was an insult. Jude had no doubt the vampire could hear the very beating of his heart. "Well, isn't that obvious? He *left!* I didn't give him permission. My master certainly didn't—*his* master, I should say. Our sire never relinquishes his property, particularly his favorite pieces."

"Property?" It was Jasper who said it, sounding every bit as horrified as Jude felt. Jude couldn't have gotten another word out to save his own life, or Pixie's. "You're a monster. You'd be a heartless monster, even if yours was still

beating."

Cruce gave a slight, casual nod, as if acknowledging a point so obvious it went without saying. "And he's a thief. Fortunately, in this case, thief and property are one and the same. Recovering one takes care of the other. Two birds, you might say." A sharp, unpleasant smile spread across his face. "And now you're here, I've got three more."

"No. It's over," Jude heard himself say. Though his insides still twisted, his voice didn't shake. He wrenched his eyes away from Pixie, forcing himself to look at the demon responsible. No, the man. Cruce was still a man and, as Eva had told him once, the worst monsters were human. "You won once, when we were scared and alone—not anymore."

"You're not alone?" Cruce grinned evilly. Vampires did indeed enjoy drama, Jude remembered the Witch saying, evidently accurately. Cultural quirk. "Good. Neither am I."

He raised one hand, and three figures stepped from the shadows behind him. Nails and Maestra stood on either side of Cruce, completely still, staring at the group of humans with unblinking, glassy eyes.

The third vampire made Jude's breath catch in his throat.

His black hair was long, unkempt where it had once been soft and glossy, partly covering his ragged face. Jude remembered hearing something about hair and nails continuing to grow after death, and wildly wondered if this was proof. His skin was a washed-out, ashen grey instead of the healthy bronze it should have been. Claws sprouted from every long, thin fingertip, and his mouth hung partly open, revealing long, deadly fangs. Huge, leathery wings were half-open behind him, brushing the ground as he moved too smoothly, too silently. Everything about him was alien, unsettlingly inhuman, wrong in the way every homo sapient instinct was programmed to fear and flee.

But his eyes were exactly the same as they'd been five years ago—and the same as they'd been hours before.

"Felix," Jasper whispered, dry voice still carrying through the vast cavern.

He tried to say something else, but all that came out was a choked sob, then silence.

Speechless, breathless, Jude noticed the Witch raise her hands from the corner of his eyes, a ball of light in each palm. He was beyond surprise. Beyond caring. He couldn't take his eyes off Felix—and, beside him, Pixie on the cross.

"Take them," Cruce said to his servants as the air began to crackle with the building magical power. "But take your time. This is going to be fun."

✸ VI THE LOVERS ✸

ACT SIX: The Circle

ONE MOMENT, the cavern was silent. The next, the air was filled with light, sound, and fury. As Cruce raised one hand with a grating laugh, Nails and Maestra rushed forward. Jude instinctively stumbled backwards, painfully aware of his fragile skin and blunt nails in the face of flashing teeth and claws. He expected the others to do the same, but Jasper didn't move. He hadn't since laying eyes on Felix, who also seemed frozen, hunched over as if making an excruciating effort to stay where he was.

The Witch, however, kept her hands raised and lights on as she stepped forward, then brought her arms down in a sweeping motion. The globes of light seemed to explode with a blinding flash that made Jude shield his eyes with one arm. There was no pain or impact, but suddenly the underground cave was as bright as a cloudless day at high noon.

Nails stopped dead, ducking her head against the glare, only for Maestra to run right into her, nearly sending both of them crashing to the ground. As the girls held onto each other to stay upright, Cruce stumbled back, shielding himself against the light with one wing.

"Felix!" he snapped, waving a hand in the Witch's direction. "Go!"

Felix took a few steps forward, then stumbled and froze again, nearly falling to his knees. His huge black wings flared out behind him, and his hands came up to clutch at his head, as if he were in excruciating pain. But he still didn't move.

For a split-second, Cruce stared at him as if unable to comprehend this unacceptable act of rebellion, but soon his astonishment became a livid snarl. "*Go!*"

Disobedience overruled, Felix surged forward in a blur, almost faster than the eye could follow—but the Witch shot forward to meet him, colliding in midair and sending both of them pitching off to the side. The monstrous-looking vampire—*Felix,* Jude reminded himself, sick—slammed back-first into the cave wall and she was on him instantly, fingernails pressed against the grey skin of his bare neck. But they somehow looked longer than they'd been a moment ago. Sharper. Like claws.

"Don't hurt him!" Jasper's desperate voice rang through the air and they both froze. Everybody did, vampires and humans, and Jude's eyes were still fixed on the Witch's hand at Felix's throat. Her fingertips did indeed end in lethal-looking claws—one twitch and they'd find out if a vampire could survive without a head.

Felix didn't strike back. Instead he seemed limp between the stone and her claws, as if she was all that kept him upright. His own clawed hands hung loose at his sides, his eyes didn't flash, and his teeth weren't bared. What Jude could see of his face behind his shaggy black hair just looked resigned. Completely at the Witch's mercy, he didn't move.

But the Witch did, whirling around with startling speed to intercept Cruce, who'd taken advantage of the standoff to sneak up behind her, bared fangs aimed right for her face. As she spun—impossibly fast, as fast as *they* moved—she threw Felix in the opposite direction, sending him flying and hitting the ground as she slammed Cruce just as hard into the wall. In a heartbeat, the Witch had him pinned against the rock, like Felix a moment before, but this time facedown. All of this in under three seconds, and she didn't look even close to breaking a sweat.

"I can't believe that worked again," she said with a rough laugh, one hand pinning his arm behind his back. It might have just been the unusual cave lighting, but now that Jude was looking for it, he could swear her skin had a grey cast to it.

"What are you?!" Cruce howled in impotent rage, struggling in vain against her iron grip. Nails, Maestra, and Felix all stared as the larger vampire fought to escape, seeming stunned and confused without his orders.

"You don't remember my name?" she snarled back, teeth snapping at his furious face. Extremely pointed teeth, Jude realized. She'd never let them show before, but now she looked like she wanted to sink them into Cruce's neck. A far cry from Pixie's small teeth-points, her canines were long and wickedly sharp, every bit as lethal as her adversary's. "You swore you'd never forget it!"

"Letizia Verazza," he grated, slowly, as her black, dully-shining, deadly-pointed claws dug into his skin. Every hair on the back of Jude's neck stood on end, and he didn't know if it was from the venom in Cruce's voice, or the wolfish smile that spread across the Witch's—Letizia's—face. Her shoulders began to shake in a silent laugh, and Jude wondered exactly how long she'd been waiting for this moment. "Slayer-witch of Venizia."

"The one and only." As his hands balled into fists, she pressed him harder against the wall. Thick, black droplets of blood, or something like it, trickled down his grey neck.

"It's been over one hundred and fifty years," he said, almost sounding pleased and excited, and Jude could swear he was actually leaning into her claws, heedless of the pain. "And you're *still* a thorn in my side."

Her eager smile showed those pointed teeth and her eyes flared in a flash of white. "Better than being a pain in the neck."

"Felix!" Cruce shouted, but Felix was bent nearly double, again seeming to struggle against an unseen but overwhelming force. He dropped to one knee, claws of one hand scraping the stone cave floor as the other one seized at his forehead. His wings flared out and rushed back in, like he was trying to throw something invisible off his back, but couldn't manage more than these

agonized spasms. Seeing no aid coming, Cruce turned his attention back to his captor, but made no move to free himself from her grasp. Instead, he casually slipped his black leather gloves off and let them drop to the ground. "Fine. I've always wanted to kill you with my bare hands anyway."

He kicked them both away from the wall, slashing at her in a frenzy. But wherever his claws raked or fangs snapped, Letizia simply wasn't there. Even when Nails and Maestra finally snapped back into action, following Cruce's commands to attack her from both sides, she evaded every blow, moving so fast she sometimes seemed to vanish entirely. Cruce pursued just as fast, faster than the human eye could easily follow, but she was always two or three steps ahead, spinning away before any of his attacks could connect, hardly seeming to touch the ground.

Jude finally forced himself to move too. Not letting himself look at the vampires' chaotic brawl, he sprinted across the cave floor to where Pixie hung from the nails in his palms.

"Pixie?" he called up, but got no response. Snarling and screeching erupted behind Jude as the fight intensified, but he couldn't look away. He couldn't get Pixie down either. He had nothing to stand on or climb up to get better access to his hands. Even if he could, the thought of hurting Pixie more was unbearable—but so was leaving him. "I'm going to get you down, don't worry."

Out of any other options or ideas, Jude positioned his shoulders under Pixie's dangling legs and feet, holding him up to provide relief to his hands, looking around desperately for help.

But everyone else was occupied. Letizia moved in an erratic flurry, throwing more occasional magical flashes which temporarily dazed her three pursuers—Cruce, Maestra and Nails were still after her, but Felix had dropped out again, this time falling to all fours. Letizia's other hand stretched toward the ceiling and, from here, Jude could see her mouthing words he couldn't hear. Again, the air felt charged, like the second before a storm. As Letizia flexed her fingers, something invisible crackled through the air, like a surge of electricity that made heads swim and hairs stand on end.

Nails stopped mid-step, frozen in place, mouth gaping, eyes wide. Maestra didn't freeze, but she stumbled and doubled over with a sharp cry, hands flying up to her head. Slowly, long braids swaying as she shook her head, she looked up, blinking as if she'd just awakened from a deep sleep and disorienting nightmare.

"Ha!" Even as Letizia feinted away from Cruce's continued strikes, she let out a triumphant laugh. Maestra, under her own power, broke pursuit and sprinted over to Nails who stood, still paralyzed, clearly fighting but unable to escape. "That's one!"

"Come on," Maestra cried, hands on Nails' cheeks, looking directly into her still-glowing eyes. "You gotta shake him off, you have to! I'm right here, I made it, you're gonna make it too!"

Cruce paused in his assault long enough to cast a furious glance at them, then back to the Witch. Letizia still had her hand raised, fingers spread as if summoning something into her grasp.

"You," he snarled, eyes flashing white. "Stealing my thralls?"

"Can't steal something that was never yours," Letizia snapped, but Cruce whirled away from her, bearing down on the still-struggling Nails. He raised his own hands, and she straightened like a marionette pulled by his strings.

But in his rush to regain control over Nails, he'd ignored Maestra—who promptly sank her teeth into his shoulder. He bellowed, but dropped Nails to the ground. In an instant, both girls sprang away from him, dancing around each other, touching each others' arms and faces as if ensuring they were both real and alive.

Once satisfied, they stopped and turned back to face Cruce, fangs bared in twin smiles.

"No!" he snapped, an edge of panic in his voice instead of rage. "I command—"

As one, they leaped upon him.

"Jasper!" Jude cried out at last, still trying to support Pixie and praying the furiously fighting vampires kept their distance. "Over here! Help!"

But Jasper didn't respond. He was standing some distance away, not nearly far enough from Cruce's slashing claws for safety, motionless, as if he'd been caught in Letizia's spell too. He stared at Felix, who'd picked himself up off the ground but still hadn't joined in the fight raging around him. His own fight seemed internal, every shred of will dedicated to the incredible effort of resisting Cruce's commands.

Jude could only watch helplessly, Pixie's feet resting on his shoulders, as Cruce leaped forward with a screech, past Felix and toward Letizia—and the lone human standing motionless in the middle of the chaos.

And still, Jasper didn't move. Neither could Jude.

But someone did. A dark shape flew into Jasper, but not to attack. In an instant, a pair of inhumanly strong, grey-skinned arms wrapped around him, pulling out of Cruce's path of destruction. As the vampires continued to fly at one another, heedless of anything else around them, Felix curled his leathery wings around Jasper, shielding him in a protective cocoon.

They stayed like that for a few seconds, blocking out everything around them, hidden from view. Then Felix unfurled his wings, pointing across the cave at Jude and Pixie. Jasper followed his direction, mouth falling open as soon as his eyes fell on them, but his eyes cleared fast, as if he'd finally remembered where he was and what needed to be done. Jasper hesitated just long enough to look into Felix's face one more time, clinging to his ragged shirt with tight fists. Then he turned and ran toward the cross.

"I can't get him down," Jude said as Jasper ran up, desperately looking up at Pixie, at a loss to do anything else and hating every moment. "I can't get Pixie down, there's nails in his hands, God, I can't—how do we do this?"

"I don't know," Jasper admitted after taking a long look, admirably calm even with the battle behind him. Or maybe just dissociating, Jude thought with a stab of unbidden envy. It was a very tempting idea. "They're certainly in deep, aren't they?"

"I—I didn't expect this," Jude stammered. "I don't have anything to get them out with! But maybe if you boost me up, I can—"

Something swooped down on the cross like an enormous bird of prey, black wings spread overhead. Jude looked up to see Felix perched atop it, his eyes fixed on Pixie in a calm focus that Jude instantly recognized, despite everything. Fangs didn't matter, or wings, or claws. This was Felix, the medic, entirely absorbed in the puzzle before him, the pause before the decisive action.

"Get ready," he said in a rough whisper, like nothing Jude remembered, but undeniably the voice he couldn't forget.

Jasper let out a small, wordless sound. Beside him, Jude was trying to form words himself, ask what he was getting ready for, but before either of them could, Felix's hands flew to Pixie's. In one fast burst of motion and smoke—his skin was *sizzling*, Jude realized, horrified—he seized the silver nail head in the center of Pixie's left hand and pulled it out, dropping it to the cave floor with a clink. His face twisted in pain, but he didn't hesitate. A second later he'd done it again, removing the second nail with his claws and a strength that made Jude dizzy to imagine. But Jude couldn't believe anything else was happening either, and all he and Jasper could do was catch Pixie as Felix carefully lowered him down.

"Thank you," Jude managed to say, still staring up at the half-human face he never thought he'd see again.

"It's not over yet," Felix answered, eyes resolved despite his still-smoking hands. Then he spread his wings and leaped from the cross back into the melee.

Cruce was outnumbered but not overpowered. With a maddened roar, he snatched Nails in one hand, flinging her away and into Maestra, who toppled right over onto the ground. Cruce staggered backwards, wavering on his feet. Something in him seemed to have snapped the moment his control over the pair was severed, leaving him somehow weakened. But like a desperate animal, even—perhaps especially—when injured, he was dangerous.

"Don't test me, you miserable little vermin," he snarled, looming over the girls with pure fury and hatred in his eyes. "I broke you once, I'll do it again! Or better yet, I'll break *him* again, and make him—"

"*No.*"Cruce barely had time to react to Felix's voice before he appeared, tackling him with a full-body slam, sending both of them somersaulting across the floor, until they came to a very sudden stop. Felix pinned the larger vampire against the wall, fangs bared, and growled his words directly into Cruce's face. *"You won't."*

Cruce smiled, seeming completely unbothered by Felix's flashing eyes, fangs, or claws. "Are you volunteering, then?"

Felix's face twisted into a monstrous grimace, something so chillingly inhuman, Jude thought, he should have been overwhelmed with terror. Should have been. Wasn't. *"I do not take orders from you."*

"Maybe not," Cruce returned, and the disturbing calm in his voice set off warning bells in Jude's mind. Cruce shoved Felix backward, flinging him away as if he weighed nothing at all. Letizia moved to pursue as Cruce blew past the freed but bewildered-looking girls. He veered into her path, dealing her a vicious shoulder-check that sent her flying. Before any of them could move, he barreled toward Jude, Jasper—and Pixie.

The impact broke Jude's grip, and he fell to the ground, slamming against the stone cave floor as Jasper did the same a few feet away. A shock of pain shot through his entire body, but all Jude could think about was Pixie, now in Cruce's grasp. *Back* in his grasp, he thought, stomach twisting as he tried to force his double-seeing eyes into focus.

"But I have *my* orders." Cruce finished, with a satisfied look down at Pixie's still-unconscious face. His huge hands kept Pixie dangling around a foot off the ground, and from where he lay, Jude could see Cruce digging in his claws. "And I can at least follow one."

As Jude struggled to his feet, he reached into his jacket pocket. There was no soft, warm bat inside this time. Instead, his hand closed over smooth, cold glass. His last hope. Pixie's last chance. If Jude didn't take this last shot right now, it wouldn't even matter; Pixie would never get to drink it, Jude would never see him again, and none of it would mean a thing.

Clarity. He'd started out facing down his nightmares in a parking lot, only comfort the satisfaction that he stood between them and his friends. Now he was doing it again. But this time, he wasn't alone—and he didn't freeze. He flung the bottle with all his strength, right toward Cruce.

It whistled as it flew through the air, turning end over end until it smacked against the huge vampire's shoulder. Cruce let out a surprised grunt and flung up one wing in a protective shield, but the glass bottle crashed to the ground and shattered, spilling red sauce across the cave floor. By the time Cruce looked up, his face had twisted into a wicked scowl, and Jude was just lowering his arm. Still hurting, still exhausted, but smiling.

"What?" Cruce scoffed, mocking laugh ringing through the vast cavern. "Was that supposed to hurt?"

"No," Jude said in a low, completely calm voice that made Cruce stop laughing immediately. Jude's heart slammed so hard his chest hurt, his ears rang, every cell in his body felt alive with terror and exhilaration and *confirmation*. This was right. This was exactly where he belonged. "It's supposed to get your attention."

Cruce snorted, glancing down at Pixie's limp form, upper lip curling to reveal his long, lethal fangs. Jude didn't flinch. He never would again. "Trying to distract me from your little friend?"

Jude smiled, and took a step back, hands raised. It was a dramatic gesture, a third-act showstopper Jasper had to be proud of, something Jude would never have attempted in his old life. The life where days stretched on without end, where nights were filled with bad dreams and waking fears, where isolation ruled, and he felt alone even standing right in front of the people he loved the most. He wasn't alone now. It felt good.

"I've got more friends than you."

Cruce followed the sweep of his arms, eyes going wide as Jude backed up to stand beside Jasper. Letizia and Felix—her steps smooth, his jerky and uncertain—moved between them and Cruce, shielding the humans. Nails and Maestra stepped forward, holding hands and eyes aglow. Slowly, the wide, mocking smile slipped from Cruce's face until he looked lost.

"So, how about it, Cruce?" Letizia's teeth snapped together as she bared them like a hungry wolf. "Do you like these odds? Seven against one, wouldn't you call that a fair fight?"

"Seven or a thousand," Cruce shot back, though his voice carried a definite note of hysteria along with the fury. "It doesn't matter! Not as long as the *one* is *me!*"

Someone started to laugh. Soft and faint. It took Jude a moment to realize where he'd heard it before and where it was coming from now. When he did, his breath caught in his throat.

"Don't you get it?" Pixie asked, smiling up into Cruce's half-livid, half-panicked face, even as his captor's hands tightened around him. "We win."

"Shut up!" Cruce's voice came out in a strangled shriek. His eyes were wide now, not luminescent. "You haven't won anything. You have no idea the Hell you'll be in, once—"

"We might not always win," Pixie said, voice growing stronger with every word and, with every word, Jude's heart beat faster. "But you'll always lose."

"*Shut up!*" Cruce shouted again, letting go of Pixie with one hand only to clamp it over his mouth. "Or I'll *make* you be quiet!"

Jude didn't need to see the lower half of Pixie's face to see his smile grow. His eyes grew brighter—not with a vampire's hostile flash, but with victory—until he jerked his head back, and sank his small fangs deep into Cruce's bare hand. The agonized, ear-splitting screech that followed was the most satisfying sound Jude had ever heard.

Cruce staggered back and Jude rushed forward. He'd spent the best years of his life running toward the flames, toward danger instead of away, and now he ran straight for the huge, furious vampire—and Pixie. Cruce's grip finally opened and he wrenched his hand away from the small, relatively dull-but-all-the-more-painful teeth, recoiling and throwing Pixie toward the ground—

Jude got there first. Pixie fell into his arms, safe at last, and Jude was sure he saw him smiling. Now he half-carried, half-dragged Pixie backwards and away from Cruce, who didn't follow. Cruce stepped backwards in the opposite direction, away from Pixie, Jude, and everyone else. His face was a mask of pure, unadulterated shock and, for the first time, Jude saw something aside from malice or cruel glee in his eyes. Fear.

Then he was gone. In his place, a huge black bat flapped in midair, before screeching and shooting away across the cavern.

"Get him!" Maestra yelled, and the girls transformed with ecstatic grins, erupting into a flurry of wings and shrieks as they pursued Cruce's flight like bats out of Hell.

Within seconds, the three of them were gone. They disappeared into shadowed tunnels across the cave, but their echoing screeches remained. Letizia and Felix made no move to follow, standing with Jude and Jasper as if they were every bit as overwhelmed and exhausted as the humans.

It was over. The air was still and Jude felt weak.

"Thank you," said Pixie, weakly curling his fingers around Jude's shirt before passing out again in his arms.

꽃

They should have been out of the caves long ago. Evil apparently vanquished, or at least driven off, there was nowhere Jude wanted to be except home, safe behind his seven locks.

But Pixie was in no condition. His scarf was missing; Jude's panicked brain latched onto that first, as before. Now, the reason Jude had never seen Pixie without it became horribly obvious. A huge, brutal-looking scar took up the entire right underside of his jaw and continuing down his neck. It wasn't a clean line, like a knife's cut. Instead, it looked like he'd been mauled by an animal, something that crushed his throat with ripping teeth. Jude felt sick just looking at it. He'd always envisioned vampire bites as relatively small, just two puncture wounds. This was something else entirely, and he couldn't stand to look for long.

As he held Pixie, Jude automatically covered the terrible scar with a hand, acutely aware of the lack of a pulse under his fingers. Pixie had always kept it hidden. He'd probably hate the idea of it being exposed right now and, somehow, covering it made Jude feel less useless. But that was far from the only problem.

The gaping wounds in Pixie's hands didn't bleed, instead oozing a thick, sluggish and black substance, like what had leaked from Cruce's neck during the battle. Even that soon stopped entirely. While brutally deep, the punctures looked almost cauterized, as if the nails that had pierced them had been red-hot. Apparently silver was another piece of the myth that was true.

He still held Jude's shirt in a weak grasp, but his eyes were shut. Jude had never seen anyone hold so still, even when sleeping. Sleeping people tended to breathe. And they were warm—so was Pixie, usually, in bat form at least. But his unhealthily-pale grey skin was cool to the touch now, and that, combined with the unnatural stillness, no breathing, no heartbeat…

For the first time, his brain understood in no uncertain terms. Pixie was dead. And if they didn't do something fast, he may somehow end up in whatever second death awaited unfortunate vampires, one from which there really was no return.

"I don't know if it's safe to move him," Jude said, own heart pounding as adrenaline continued to surge through his veins. He knew this feeling, holding someone possibly grievously injured in his arms, and being so afraid of making it worse. He'd been here before. Last time it had been Jasper, as a fire raged around them. Now, there were no flames or smoke, and Jasper was right here with him. And Felix, whose presence Jude could barely wrap his head around, who'd yet to leave Jasper's side. He also had yet to venture close enough to Jude to touch, or even meet his eyes for more than a half-second, and that alone gave Jude a cold pang of distress. But now wasn't the time, he looked as worried as Jude felt, and none of it gave Pixie a better chance of survival. "He doesn't look good at all."

"I can hear you..." Pixie shifted slightly, and Jude let out a rush of breath, a wave of relief shaking him to his core. He didn't open his eyes, and his words came out in an almost-unintelligible mumble, but with an accompanying ear twitch as if to demonstrate.

"He needs to feed," Letizia said without pretense, a rare urgency in her usually-languid voice. "Any of us would after what he's been through. Or even a lot less for that matter."

Jude shot an increasingly anxious look at the red spatter across the cave floor, dried and useless. "I brought sauce, but the bottle shattered when I threw it. It was all I could think to do, I'm sorry!"

"S'fine," Pixie murmured, words barely audible and lips barely moving. He slowly opened his eyes, blinking a few times in what seemed like an exhausting effort, and gave Jude a weak smile. "Don't worry about it."

"You're not fine!" Jude's voice came out higher than intended, with a definite edge of panic. "You were almost—you just really need blood. It heals you, right? That's what you need right now?"

"Not gonna..." Pixie started, then trailed off, seeming to forget what he'd been in the middle of saying. His words came out slurred and halting and his eyes drifted out of focus. "Mm-mmnnnn."

"I can do it," Jasper said in a low but determined voice, with a matching expression of grim resolve. "I've done it before."

Pixie shook his head and made a distressed, protesting noise, and Jude felt much like doing the same. But that wouldn't solve anything, the only thing that would help was figuring this out, fast, and he desperately cast about for a solution.

"If we can just get him back to my place, there's more there—or somebody can run back and get it. You," he said, looking up at Letizia, aware of the obvious worry on his face and not caring. "If I give you the key, can you fly back to my apartment and get the sauce from the fridge? Wait, do you need me to invite you in? Can I do that from here, just give you permission now?"

"I could," she said, voice and expression grave. "And it wouldn't take long. But I still don't know what condition he'll be in by the time I get back. He needs help, now, and we're lucky anyone here can give it to him. What's your answer?"

Jude didn't give one for a few seconds, or even move. He knew the answer, but couldn't bring himself to say it. After every surreal thing out of his dreams and nightmares, even after the fight against a monster, even seeing Felix, returned but transformed, this was somehow on another level. When Jude had started his quest for answers—no, his vendetta, really, against all things fanged... *this* had been out of the question. The one thing he swore would never happen, the line he'd never cross. It should have been simple, but nothing was.

His eyes went again to Pixie's neck, the terrible, animal-attack-looking scar his hand almost covered, but not quite. Was that what vampires really did to people? To each other? Was that what Pixie was going to—

"Jude. We don't have time for this," Jasper prodded, grave voice bringing him back to the present. "I'm not sure Pixie does either."

He did know one simple thing: if their positions were reversed, Pixie would save Jude's life without question. He wouldn't even have hesitated this long. Jude knew that like he knew the full moon meant trouble, and guitars killed fascists. He knew it like he knew Eva's steady eyes and Jasper's quick smile. Like Felix's warm voice. He knew it like he knew he'd been right for so many years about everything and finally been vindicated—almost everything. He'd been wrong about one thing. One person. And here he had the chance to be right again.

"Okay," Jude said, voice and hands steady, and rolled up his sleeve. "Pixie?"

He didn't get an answer. Pixie's eyes were shut and face slack, even his ears were still. He had slipped back into unconsciousness. Jude gave him a gentle shake, as much as he dared, but he didn't move. Jude felt a stab of panic in his chest and let out a swear under his breath. "He's not—what do I do? I don't know how to—"

"Do you trust him?" It wasn't Jasper who spoke, but Letizia, appearing at Jude's elbow as if out of nowhere.

"What?"

As Jude stared at her, she held up one finger, light catching her black, curved claw. "I won't ask you to trust me, you've got no reason to. It's not about me anyway. Do you trust him?"

Jude didn't hesitate. He never would again. "Yes."

"Then give me your arm," she said, sounding perfectly reasonable and businesslike. "One small cut, I promise. That's all he'll need. It might sting, but not for long. Vampire saliva has a numbing effect."

"This is really happening," Jude murmured, holding out his arm but keeping his eyes on Pixie. He had to be doing the right thing. Everything had led to this. They'd faced monsters and traumatic memories, they'd made a deal and worked together beyond the terms and conditions. Somewhere along the way, Jude had started to trust him, look over his shoulder, or feel for the soft warmth of a bat in his pocket, and be relieved to find Pixie still there. This had to be the right thing. He had to still be there when this was over. "This is—ah!"

It did sting. But it really was only one small and shallow cut, a single, fast swipe from her claw across his skin. It didn't even bleed nearly as much as he expected—but Pixie's eyes still snapped open, black pupils round and huge, with barely a bit of brown and white around the edges. As he stared, wide-eyed at the small trickle of red on Jude's forearm, he started to shake, hands curled into fists. But he didn't move, seeming paralyzed, caught between an instinctual desire and abject terror of following it.

"It's okay," Jude said, meaning every syllable and wondering exactly when all his doubts had been replaced by such certainty. "You're okay. I give you permission."

Pixie's feverish eyes were filled with a combination of anxiety and hope and, when they flicked up to meet Jude's, he held out his arm and nodded confirmation. Pixie didn't lurch or spring forward, instead sitting up just enough to reach and, when his mouth closed over the cut, he didn't bite down at all. Jude felt weak with relief. No fangs. Even after all this, he'd been expecting something aggressive, something terrifying, ripping teeth and dizzying pain. He'd been ready for something like the attack that had ravaged Pixie's neck. But what he got was soft, warm, entirely unlike a bite and so much more like a kiss.

As it went on, Jude slowly felt his own tense muscles relax. He didn't know when he'd slipped one hand under Pixie's head to support him and make the angle less awkward, but he knew, like everything else in this moment, it had been the right thing.

Jude's primary attention remained on Pixie, but he was aware of the others behind him, softly talking amongst themselves. It was comforting, a reminder that he wasn't alone, even if he couldn't bring himself to join.

"Thank you," Jasper said in a quiet, awed voice. He still held Felix's hand, gently avoiding the smoking welts, and stared at it as he spoke. "For sparing Felix."

"It was the least I could do," Letizia said with a one-shouldered shrug, as if she'd just picked up something on his grocery list. "I mean that. The very least."

"You could have hurt him." Jasper gave his head a slow shake. He moved it gingerly, haltingly, sure signs that it was starting to give him trouble again. "Easily, from the look of it. Thank you for freeing him instead."

"I saw the way you looked at him." Letizia gave a slow smile, starkly different from her usual smirk. "Like he's all that matters in the world. Like he *is* the world. I looked at someone like that once."

Jasper started to reply, but the moment he looked back at Felix, words seemed to fail. He just looked at him, making no effort to wipe away the fresh tears that spilled from his eyes. One hand went to the back of his head and neck, as if the pain were intensifying, but he didn't look away. Felix's eyes followed the motion, widening in something that looked like mingled recognition and concern. He raised one grey, burned hand as well, and slowly, gently, laid it on Jasper's head where he'd started rubbing. Jasper drew in a shuddering gasp at the touch, eyes wide and mouth slightly open, as if he were witnessing something inexpressibly transcendent. He leaned into Felix's hand, closed his eyes, and was silent.

"Thanks from me too," Pixie said then, carefully withdrawing from Jude's arm and weakly swiping at his mouth until no trace of red remained. The cut on Jude's arm didn't bleed nearly as much as he'd imagined, and in fact seemed to be scabbing over now that Pixie was done—which he seemed to be, eyeing the cut but making no move toward it. His voice was still faint, but he seemed to have recovered a great deal from even a small amount of blood. When he opened his eyes, they were clear, and his pupils weren't quite as blown out. "To both of you. Felix…"

The other vampire didn't speak, or remove his hand from Jasper's head. Slowly, he looked over at Pixie, looking almost afraid of what he might hear, as well as deeply ashamed. Jude's heart ached to see that expression on Felix's face. But there seemed to be no blame on Pixie's side, nothing but the same warmth and gratitude he'd given the others.

"Felix was there the night I got taken. The whole time, actually." As Pixie spoke, Felix's shoulders sagged and his head dropped until it hung low, once-smooth black hair hiding his face in a tangled curtain. Until now his wings had hung half-open behind him, but now they came up, curling around himself as if he wanted to hide behind them. "No, no, don't feel bad! He helped me escape," Pixie said quickly, looking up at the others as if to make sure nobody doubted it. Once satisfied, he turned back to Felix. "And you weren't doing any of it because you wanted to. Believe me, I know. Cruce's bad enough on his own, but he's nothing compared to what you… what *we*…

I just know you didn't have a choice. It's okay."

There was something behind that, Jude thought, remembering Cruce's words about orders, his master. The implication filled him with foreboding but with Pixie barely recovering and clearly having difficulty talking about it, now didn't seem like the time to bring an all-new horror. Jude didn't ask the question on his mind, but he'd save it for later.

Felix didn't answer either. Instead he gave Pixie a slow nod, then shut his eyes, gently leaning against Jasper and looking more exhausted than anyone Jude had ever seen, living, dead, or otherwise.

"I just can't believe this is happening," Jasper said, smiling through his tears. He'd told Jude not long ago that for the first time in years, Jude seemed alive. Amazingly, the same seemed to be true of him. "We have to tell Eva! As soon as we can—if that's all right with you?" Felix nodded without hesitation, and Jasper smiled, looking more blissful than he had in five years or longer. "Then it's settled. We'll have our lives back. Or even better, new ones."

"Wait, I'm not sure about this," Jude said, hesitating as he felt the full weight of not just all that had happened, but all that he'd denied. There was so much he hadn't been able to tell her—partly because she hadn't wanted to hear it, hadn't been ready. How could anybody be ready? Still, as he imagined actually revealing everything, no emotion rose so strongly to the surface as guilt. "This is just a lot to take in all at once, and she doesn't know anything about this. Maybe we should wait—what?"

Letizia gave a snort and he looked up in time to catch the vaguely annoyed look on her face. "Unbelievable."

"Listen," Jude said, with what he felt was admirable patience, half-turning to face her without letting go of Pixie. "I'm grateful for your help, really. We appreciate it. But you don't know us, and you don't know Eva."

"I know what it's like to lose a friend." Letizia folded her arms and stared Jude down; he suppressed a shiver at her hard, unyielding eyes. Cruce had called her a slayer-witch. He thought he'd been a hunter, or at least working to become one. But he knew the real thing when he saw it, and knew he'd never compare. "And I know what I'd do if I thought it would bring them back. Shouldn't yours at least get that choice?"

In the awkward silence that followed, Jude peered into the shadowy tunnel entrances around the cavern, pointing his thumb in the direction Nails and Maestra had disappeared in their pursuit. "Are they coming back?"

It was a weak subject change, but Letizia seemed content to take it. "They deserve a free flight," she said, face softening slightly and reverting to her customary smirk. "And the chance to chase Cruce—even if they won't catch him. Still," she said, taking a step away from the group. "I'd better go make sure they don't run into any more trouble. The world's unfriendly to baby vampires."

Again, there was no sound or magical flash. She was simply there one second and gone the next. Confused, Jude looked around for the bat he now expected to appear whenever this happened, but there was none. Letizia had simply disappeared.

"She likes drama, doesn't she?" he asked, turning to Jasper to find him actually smiling.

"I believe witches enjoy it just as much as vampires. And some people happen to be both."

Jude shook his head and gave a soft laugh. It felt good. "How are we doing?"

"I have everything," Jasper said, looking down at Felix's burned hand in his own as if he still couldn't believe it. Felix still didn't speak, but he nodded and pulled Jasper closer, reaching out with one wing to gently encircle him in its black, leathery-looking folds. "I'm never letting go. And it looks like I'm not the only one." Jasper nodded down at Pixie, still held safely in Jude's arms, and raised his eyebrows so far they almost disappeared into his hair. Jude probably would have gotten his point anyway.

"It's about time we all went home," he said instead of answering Jasper's hint, eyebrows coming together as he warily took in Felix's ragged clothes, grey skin, long and untended hair, claws, and wings. "But how are we going to get them there? It should still be night, the mall's closed, but what if someone's hanging around?"

"I can just bat again," Pixie offered, with an only slightly-loopy-sounding giggle. He was sounding stronger all the time, but still nowhere near actually walking anywhere. "You still got pockets, right?"

"Yeah, I've got—fine," Jude said, steadfastly ignoring the heat rising in his cheeks. "You do that. Felix, can you... bat?"

Felix was silent for a few seconds, looking at the ground with such a deeply ashamed expression it made Jude's heart ache. Having Felix back, only to see that kind of pain on his face, was almost more than he could stand. Finally, he spoke, voice faint and rasping, so rough it sounded painful.

"I can't transform. Either way. Bat or human. I'm stuck between. I'm sorry."

"Hush about that," Jasper said without hesitation. "You have nothing to apologize for, or worry about. We'll get you home and worry about the rest later." Felix didn't look convinced, but Jasper did, smiling. "Do you know, walking down the street with you is the one part of this I'm not worried about? I've seen stranger-looking people by far, every day. And that's in broad daylight—such that it is in Portland, another unexpected bonus."

"We do kind of fit in here." Pixie gave a lopsided grin that made Jude's anxious heart feel a little lighter, a little warmer. "Just keeping it weird."

🔥

Jude wanted to call Eva right away. He'd wanted to the moment he got home, but Pixie asleep on his couch and every window in the apartment covered with towels and duct tape would have raised too many questions that he didn't know how to answer. And Jude wasn't about to move him.

Jasper had taken Felix back to his place and Jude had reluctantly let them go—taking his eyes off Felix was almost physically painful, but then, so was looking at him. And Felix hadn't been able to look at him fully yet at all. Was he too ashamed of his new, half-transformed appearance? Had he heard Jude was supposed to be a hunter—was he actually afraid? Either possibility was unthinkable. Jude wanted to follow them, stay looking, stay touching, stay close, even if regaining whatever they'd once had might be impossible. But that would have left Pixie alone and that was definitely impossible.

Jude didn't quite know what to do with himself. For once, he had no driving urge to hit the dark streets and root out fanged threats, especially when almost every vampire he'd met recently had turned out to be much less threatening than he'd expected. Glad as he was that the fight was over, the hunt itself had given his life purpose and direction. Where did he go from here? He didn't know. For the first time, he had options, and that was overwhelming. Still, he couldn't just sit here in a dark room and do nothing. He'd never been good at that, and there was someone he still badly needed to talk to. As a few rays of sunlight just barely started to peek through gaps he'd missed, he picked up the phone.

It only rang once.

"Eva? It's—"

"Jude! God, it's good to hear your voice." Her relief was palpable and she spoke fast, as if galvanized into a second wind after a long, exhausting night. "I checked your place a couple times and you weren't there—I was literally just about to walk out the door to check again. If you weren't there I was going to call the police. When did you get back?"

"Late," he said, realizing he didn't specifically know what time. Before sunrise, thankfully. "Really late. I'm sorry for making you worry."

"It's fine," she said, in the quick, light tone that suggested that it wasn't fine, but acknowledged that neither of them had the energy to analyze it yet. "Did you get him back?"

Jude nodded. Then, upon realizing foggily that people couldn't generally see through phones, he made himself talk. "Yeah. Yes, Pixie's fine—or he will be, I think. He's actually sleeping here, I've got him on my couch."

"Sounds like he had a rough night."

"Yeah," Jude sighed. He may have been sleepwalking for five years, never fully awake, but it didn't feel like he'd slept in that long either. Sleeping for five more years was starting to sound pretty good. "We… yeah, it was. Really rough."

Eva was silent on the other end of the line. Jude couldn't even hear her breathing. She was going to ask him to take her through it. Exactly who'd kidnapped Pixie and why—he'd managed to avoid saying the 'V' word last night, though it had been heavily implied. She'd accepted it then, but now? It was daylight, she was about to ask directly, and Jude was out of excuses. He had to tell her the truth.

Finally, she broke the silence, but it wasn't to ask the question turning his insides to ice. "So, that sounds like the good news."

"What?" he frowned; she'd veered off-course. This wasn't turning out like he'd rehearsed it in his head.

"Getting Pixie back. Everything turning out okay. That's the good news, right? So what's the bad news?" Eva prodded, sounding a little afraid to hear the answer. "You're holding something back, you're scared to tell me because it's really bad, or you think I'll think you're crazy, or back on your vampire bullshit. And you don't have to. Not from me."

"You can tell that, huh?" He leaned against the wall, letting his head tip back and eyes slip shut.

"You're not that subtle, Jude." Eva paused. When she spoke again she sounded as hesitant, anxious, and exhausted as he felt. "It's something new, isn't it? Usually you're not exactly quiet about… things. If it was just, uh, the usual, I can't imagine you holding back."

"Neither can I," he said with a tired smile, and a just-as-tired but true rush of affection. How well did she know him? How was it that some people just worked themselves into the patchwork of your life, until it felt like they'd always been there? That memories without them seemed empty, even if they outnumbered the years they'd been together? That the time before knowing them felt like a life belonging to someone else?

"So what *are* you holding back?" she prodded. And how well did he know her? She just wouldn't be Eva if she let it go. They were the same that way. Always had been.

"Holding back?" He sucked in a breath. Held it. Let it go. "Yeah. I am. I'm just trying to figure out how to say it in a way that doesn't freak either of us out."

"But it's not working?"

"Not really, no."

"Then why don't you just say it now and we freak out later?" Her tone sounded half-joking but he could hear the tension, the same anxiety that made it feel like his stomach was eating him from the inside out.

"Because… it's not the kind of thing you want to hear over the phone."

"What happened?" She'd dropped all attempts at lightness and now the fear was undisguised.

"We're fine," he said quickly. "Nobody's—Jasper and I are fine, I promise. I wouldn't keep that from you."

"I know," she said with a fast exhale. "But just checking."

"Yeah." He shot a glance at Pixie, still on his couch, still asleep. Not moving. Jude headed into his room and shut the door, hoping it would be enough to keep his lowered voice from reaching those big, pointed ears. Pixie needed the rest. "Can we talk at your place?"

"Sure," Eva said, sounding remarkably calm, considering. "I was going to take today off anyway. Mental health day."

"Okay. Give me five minutes."

"Five minutes."

"Yeah. And Eva—thank you."

Jasper took a much longer time to pick up the phone than Eva had, long enough Jude had started pacing, then made himself stop, worried about waking Pixie. He restricted his nervous motion to folding his arms and drumming his fingers against his elbow.

"Hello?"

"Jasper?" Jude said immediately, trying to keep his voice down to a whisper and mostly succeeding.

"Speaking." He sounded like he'd just woken up. Jude felt a pang of jealousy, both for the sleep, and the image currently floating around his head. He'd woken Jasper up enough times to know what that voice meant. Jude was an early riser even on weekends, while Jasper and Felix were decidedly not.

"I told Eva," he blurted at last. "Not everything—but I'm going to. It's time, past time, she deserves to know."

"Right now?" Jasper sounded slightly more awake, or at least alarmed.

"I'm going upstairs," Jude said, surprised at the resolve in his own voice. "I'm going to talk to her first, and then…"

"You want us to come in?"

Jude froze. It wasn't Jasper's voice that had finished the thought.

"Felix?" When Jude finally found his own voice, it came out in a breathless whisper. Somehow this still felt like a dream. Like any moment, the past several days would be erased, leaving Jude's world as it had been.

"Hey, Jude."

The world shrank. The universe fell silent. Nothing existed except the phone in his hand, and the voice coming from it, the words he'd never expected to hear again and feel anything but pain. Jude half-leaned, half-fell against the wall, eyes shut and mouth open, letting out a sound somewhere between a laugh and a sob. It felt like the Earth had just pitched beneath his feet, knocking him off-balance. But instead of falling, he was weightless. He may never touch the ground again. Eyes stinging, he made himself answer. "*Hey.*"

There was a long silence. Jude focused on getting his breath back and rubbed at his wet eyes. Finally, Felix continued, sounding so apprehensive, so anxious, so unlike he'd ever been, the laid-back calm and teasing medic forever preserved in Jude's memory. "Are you sure it's a good idea for… I'm… I just don't want to scare her."

"That's why I want to go first. I'll let Eva know you're alive, just a little different than she knew you." Hopefully he'd just imagined Felix's mirthless, bitter laugh after the word 'alive.'

"A little, yes." Definitely a laugh, but not a sarcastic one as he'd feared. It sounded painful, but, like the words only he could get away with even after all these years, it was *him*. So unmistakably familiar, so unmistakably Felix, underneath it all. "Tell her… I can't wait to see her. I missed her."

Jude smiled, praying he was up to any of this. Out of everything they'd been through, this next step seemed like the most perilous. And the most important. "Tell her yourself."

🔥

Eva was almost as fast opening her door as she was picking up the phone. Jude had barely knocked once before it flew open and he found himself pulled into a tight hug, the air rushing from his lungs in a not-unpleasant way.

"Thank God," Eva murmured into his shoulder before pushing back to hold him at arm's length, taking a good look into his face. "You're really okay? Everything all in one piece?"

Jude tried to smile. The pain in his leg had faded, phantom and otherwise, and he'd even managed to escape without any new scars. The past few days had been harrowing, but all in all, he'd emerged in much better condition than he might have. Maybe there *were* other scenarios besides worst-case ones. "As much as ever."

"Good. Okay. So," she stepped back inside, nodding for him to follow as she did whenever he actually came over. He'd done that more than usual since all this started, he realized. It had almost been… nice. Maybe the next time he came to see her wouldn't involve vampires or any other sources of potential doom. "Under the mall. Pixie getting kidnapped—by who?"

"Um," he stopped mid-step, stomach clenching despite his dedication to see this through. He tried an old grounding exercise: pick an object in the room and study it, describe it mentally, even a wall or floor. Her hardwood was a lot cleaner than his, even after he'd swept up a lot of dust along with the glass from his broken window. It looked like she actually cleaned it, did some kind of wood treatment to make it shine. She did that, always put real effort and attention to detail in everything she did. Eva gave everything she had. It was time she got something in return. "I don't know, exactly. A really bad guy—at least one. But that's not what I wanted to talk to you about."

"Oh, really?" she shot him a smile that looked half-amused, half-resigned. "What's bigger news than foiling a kidnapping in a secret underground?"

Jude had never been good at conversation. Smoothness, tact, clever phrase-turns, those were Jasper's department, and Jude could never hope to compare. Especially not about something so important. So he just said it: one small word for him, one giant leap for all of their lives. "Felix."

The smile slipped off Eva's face. "What?"

Jude took a deep breath, held it. Felt the air in his lungs, held onto this moment, of holding absolutely still. Of standing on a threshold. Hanging, hesitating just before that no-return step, a second of unbroken stillness and clarity in which he could spend a lifetime. He'd been on this threshold for five years. Then, as he had so often the past several nights, Jude made himself keep going. "He's alive."

"Fe…" Eva stopped, staring at Jude, eyes wide and round, and face uncomprehending—until her head slowly began to shake. "No."

"Yes. Yes, he is. I…" Jude realized he was nodding, as if trying to convince himself of the same idea he could see Eva fighting herself to believe. "I know how it sounds—believe me, I know, it's impossible, it has to be a lie, or a trick, or just a really, really bad joke, except that out of anything else in the world, I wouldn't joke about this."

"Y-you don't joke about anything," she stammered, an uneasy smile flickering across her face. There was the lightheadedness, the this-isn't-really-happening, everything's-kind-of-funny feeling. He was getting too good at recognizing it.

"I know," he said, grounding himself, keeping his voice level so maybe he could do the same for her. "But even if I did, I wouldn't about this. I said I'd never lie to you again, and I wasn't lying then either."

"Felix...?" She held absolutely still. Her smile was gone, replaced by an expression he half-knew. He recognized the desperation and near-panic. He'd seen it often enough in the mirror, and been the cause of it too much for her. But the other half, the fragile openness of her wide eyes and held breath took him a moment to identify. Hope.

"Look in my eyes, Eva." Gently, he reached out to take both of her hands, but kept his eyes on her face, and she never once looked away. "I'm telling you the truth. He's alive."

She stared at him for what felt like hours. Finally, she recovered enough to form one word. "How?"

"It's..." Jude stopped, scrambling for words and coming up empty. 'Long story' didn't begin to cover it. And he wished he had another one to tell, one that Eva had a better chance of believing. But there was no other explanation, and she'd see for herself soon. "He's not quite the same as he was."

"What does that mean?" she asked, suspicion re-entering her tone for the first time. He could feel her building up her walls, preparing for more pain and disappointment. It was what happened every time he'd tried to talk to her before. She withdrew and denied out of self-preservation, he kept pushing, and they never took a step forward. But this couldn't be like that, they couldn't go through the same motions and go nowhere. This time would be different.

"This is why I didn't want to tell you over the phone," he said quickly, trying to get the words out before she retreated too far away. "You need to see him."

"See him," she whispered. The distance fell away. Jude let himself hope.

"They'll be here in a few minutes. Jasper's bringing him." He stopped to swallow hard and check her face for disbelief or panic, but she wasn't looking at him anymore. Eva's eyes were unblinking, gazing past him, over his shoulder to her front door. "But before they get here, you have to know a few things."

"What?" she asked faintly, wavering a little on her feet. "What things?"

"Do you need to sit down?" Jude tried to take her by the arm and lead her over to the couch, but she shook him off, and stood firm.

"What *things*, Jude?" Eva asked, looking back at him now, eyes clear and focused. Ready to break away at the first sign of his old bullshit. Ready to take on whatever she heard. But he'd seen the fatigue and fragile trust in her eyes, and prayed that when he said the words she needed to hear, she'd hear the truth in them. "What do I need to know?"

"A lot's happened over the last five years," he said, words coming out faster as his heart started to pound. Any minute now. "And he's gone through some changes. The kind of changes that... I've been talking about. Ever since."

"Are you saying," she said slowly. Jude could practically feel her slipping into a state he knew all too well, the dissociation that had nearly become his default. "That Felix is a vampire? Is that what you're telling me right now?"

"I'm telling you that it's still him, Eva," Jude said, as simply and honestly as he knew how. "Just, no matter what he looks like, remember that it's still him."

Eva opened her mouth but no sound came out. Before she could say a word, there was a soft knock at the door. She seemed frozen, rooted to the spot, unable to move or speak. Jude knew from experience that she was caught in one of those year-seconds, time meaningless and breaking free impossible. So he took a small step toward her and spoke in a low voice.

"We don't have to do this now," he said. "I can tell them to wait. It's a lot to take in, we shouldn't be springing this on—"

"No," Eva said abruptly. She didn't look at him, eyes still fixed on the door, but there was no shake in her voice. "I want to know. All this time I've wanted to know, I need answers just as much as you do, I just..."

"I know." Jude gave her a faint smile. "It's a lot."

"Yeah," she agreed with a slow nod. "But I'm ready. Been ready. It's open," she called, raising her voice. It still didn't shake or crack, but Jude knew that familiar mixture of terror and hope when he heard it.

The door opened, and Jasper stepped through, giving Jude a quick, bright smile, and Eva a more bittersweet one. For the first time in recent memory, he said nothing.

Behind him stood a taller figure dressed all in black. Felix did not move to step inside, and Jude could see that he stood outside the doorway, just past the threshold. Today he wore a long black trenchcoat, the odd shape of which told Jude that he'd folded his wings tight across his back, but they weren't meant to lie completely flat. His hair was at least neater than it had been last night, combed out of his eyes at least and only slightly shaggy instead of the mess it had been. Eva's eyes swept over him once, twice, flicked over to Jasper, then Jude, as if making sure they weren't playing an elaborate trick on her—then right back to his face.

"Felix?" she whispered, eyes so wide and round the whites stood out all around her pupils. There were tears spilling from them before the word even left her lips.

"Eva..." his voice was soft. Softer than it had been on the phone; Jude had the impression he was trying to keep the edges of roughness or distortion out. "It's me," he said as Jasper quietly slipped over to stand next to Jude, giving Eva and Felix the moment. Felix's voice was still raspy from disuse but sounding a little clearer every time. He also spoke without moving his lips much and Jude could easily guess why, remembering the flash of his fangs. "I'm... I missed you."

Jude couldn't help smiling as Felix took his suggestion to tell Eva himself, and saw the clear gratitude in the brief glance Felix shot his way. Eva didn't react. She never looked away from Felix's face, not for a moment. She didn't reply either, just holding perfectly still, staring into his eyes, mouth hanging open. Silence stretched, until, finally, Felix broke it.

"May I come in?"

"What?" Eva whispered, blinking as if the question was in another language, one neither of them spoke. Then she nodded, and kept nodding as she stared, eyes sweeping over him, from his grey face to his bare, clawed feet. They must have been impossible to fit into any shoes Jasper had. "Yes. I mean, please, yes… come in."

After only the barest hesitation, he took a step, crossing the threshold. As Felix's face broke into a relieved smile, Eva took one slow step forward of her own. Then two much faster ones, and Felix barely had time to open his arms before she fell into them.

She let out a strangled, pained sound Jude had never heard from her before, or anything that came close. Felix stood with his arms awkwardly held out to either side, as if he was afraid to touch and accidentally hurt her and, as Eva sobbed unabashedly into his chest, Jude had the dim realization that he couldn't remember the last time he'd seen Eva cry. If ever. But she was crying hard now, like some dam had finally burst, a release too powerful to hold back another second. And slowly, carefully, Felix wrapped his arms around her, shoulders and head dropping as if he'd been carrying a crushing weight for years and finally let it go.

"I'm so sorry," he said at last, a whisper barely audible over Eva's sobs.

"For what?" Eva asked, not letting him go or even looking up. "You didn't do anything. *I'm* sorry for—God, all this time? You were dead. I swear to God, you were dead, I never would have given up if I'd thought for a minute…"

"No," Felix said quietly as she trailed off, words dissolving into tears again. "I'm sorry for the time you had to hurt. Five years. For then, and now." He spoke in short, careful sentences, as if he were choosing his words with the greatest of care, maybe to avoid being misunderstood, or preserve his almost certainly still-aching vocal cords. "How I am now."

"I don't care!" she said immediately, only pulling him closer. "I don't care how you are, just that you *are*—that's not true, of course I care, I need answers, but right now? You're here. Everything else is icing!"

"Still," he said, an actual smile spreading across his face, one that Eva looked up just in time to catch. The dryness in his tone had nothing to do with his neglected voice, nor did the ironic glint Jude caught in his eye. In that moment, the new Felix looked so much like his old self it hurt. In a good way. "This has to be a surprise."

"I've had bigger," Eva said, shaking her head. The sob that came after was at least half-laugh. "And a lot worse. This—this is nothing."

"There's so much I want to say." Felix looked up at Jude as Eva leaned in for another hug and stayed there. Even though his eyes looked more feline than human, they were as expressive as they'd been in life, and Jude could see his struggle to find words that remained stubbornly out of reach. "To all of you. So much. I don't know where to start."

"So don't start," Eva said, voice a little muffled with half her face still pressed against Felix's chest. His arms were around her again, with only a half-second hesitation this time. "You're here. That's enough for right now. More than enough."

"Okay," he whispered, eyes still locked on Jude's, still looking caught between joy and disbelief. "I'll explain everything later. You'll get your answers. Promise."

Eva still didn't let Felix go, but Jude caught the smile on her face. Just for a moment it was aimed at him. "You'd better."

🔥

Jude was tired and overwhelmed, as he frequently was. But he was overwhelmed in a good way, which occurred much less frequently. Eva took most of the news like a champ, though she'd obviously need some adjustment time. Once everything was out in the open, she and Jude had gotten about as far as "Can you believe it?" "No, but it's happening," before they ran out of words. There was too much to say, and not enough words to say it. Not yet. They all needed to find their equilibrium and it couldn't be rushed.

So Jude let Eva process and left Felix and Jasper to sleep, wrapped up in each other. They'd stay that way for days on end or, at least, that's what he imagined and hoped. He had so much he wanted to say to Felix and could tell the feeling was absolutely mutual, desperately so—but this couldn't be rushed either. Felix seemed to have an easier time talking to Jasper, and Jude got the feeling he needed time to work up to addressing Jude directly. They'd get there. He had to believe that.

Jude didn't want to intrude, on them or Eva, so he used the time trying to find his own solid ground—and he always did that best alone. And he *was* alone. After he'd recovered enough, Pixie had said he had some thinking to do and unspecified 'things' to see about. Jude could relate, but still felt a pang of anxiety and something harder to define as Pixie left—out the door this time, not the window.

Anticlimactic, Jude reflected, leaning back in the chair Pixie's first entrance had overturned. He stared up at the white plaster ceiling, counting the dents left by the broom-handle that came in handy whenever his upstairs neighbor cranked up the volume. Pixie wouldn't live upstairs from him again, at least not without raising some very awkward questions. It would be a lot quieter around here.

That thought didn't make Jude nearly as happy as it might have once.

Their deal was over. They'd done what they'd agreed. The major vampiric threat was vanquished and the not-so-monstrous monsters wreaking havoc in the mall had been freed. Stigmata scars and traumatic memories aside, the venture had been pretty successful. And now, Jude and Pixie's temporary alliance was…

Did it really have to be temporary? Why should they go back to being strangers, or passing acquaintances? Jude had never been great at expressing himself. But of all the difficult words in the world, the one giving him the most trouble was goodbye.

A quiet tapping interrupted his melancholy thoughts, and he turned—not toward the door, but the window. It was still broken. He'd duct-taped cardboard across the frame as well as he could, but it let in a substantial draft. Below his improvised fix, he could see a few inches of light cast by the streetlamp outside, and a small bit of pink fluff and peach-fuzzy wings.

Jude bit down on his lips to keep from smiling as he stepped over and lifted the makeshift window. It actually did open, but it was far from perfect. Sometimes you didn't need perfect, he thought, looking down at the pink bat on the windowsill. And sometimes you didn't recognize it at first, even when it was right in front of you.

"Hello," he said as the bat wiggled over the window threshold and onto the inner sill. "I heard that. Another crash landing?"

"Nah, I just thought I'd actually knock this time." Pixie replied, once he was human enough to speak. He smiled, but looked a little apprehensive as he precariously balanced half-in, half-out of the window, feet not touching the floor. He wore a new scarf around his neck—red this time, and made from a shiny silk or silk-like material. Jude could swear he'd seen it somewhere before. "Can I come in?"

"You're mostly in already," Jude observed, unable to keep the smile off his face entirely. He didn't expect to feel a wave of relief on seeing a vampire in his window, but he hadn't expected a lot of things lately. "Does it even matter if I say no?"

"Course it does." Pixie said immediately. He looked and sounded like his usual upbeat self but, by now, Jude recognized the seriousness and slight anxiety in his eyes. He looked mostly recovered from his ordeal under the mall, but Jude could still easily see white, starburst-shaped scars on the backs of both hands. "I gotta be invited, remember?"

"Didn't I already?" Jude was surprised at the teasing note in his own voice, and the second laugh that wanted to escape him when Pixie gave him a surprised look, long ears twitching. It was cute. Jude didn't use that descriptor often, but couldn't think of a better one. "I distinctly remember saying something like that when we came here after that night in the parking lot."

"Well… yeah," Pixie said after hesitating. He was definitely nervous, and Jude didn't feel like teasing him anymore. "But there's saying something in, like, the heat-of-the-moment, and then there's what you really want."

"What I really want?" Jude repeated, more to himself than Pixie. He was still getting acquainted with the idea, especially when, like closure and perfection, he didn't recognize it at first. Even when it was right in front of him.

"Yeah." Pixie looked up at him, eyes wide but expression relatively reserved, likely his attempt at a pokerface. "Back then, I was hurt and we were scared and you said 'stay with me.' So I did. But just 'cause you said yes one time doesn't mean it's okay every time."

Jude started to nod and give his assent, when he stopped, something occurring to him. Like the idea of Felix at his door, he found this one unexpected, exciting, and a little bit paralyzing. Still, as he'd done so much in his life, Jude forced himself to keep moving forward. "This isn't just a vampire thing, is it?"

"No," Pixie said, voice small and surprisingly trepidatious, as if a single word from Jude would be enough to bring him to life or extinguish it for good. "It's a... wanting to stay here and hang out with you thing. But not if you don't want me to. You don't have to say yes, really, I just thought—"

"Pixie..." Jude said, voice quiet but sure. "Come in. You are hereby invited."

"Okay." There was no broken glass on the floor this time, but Pixie still stepped down carefully, seeming relieved and a little in awe to be back in Jude's apartment. Jude recognized the deer-in-the-headlights look, the one that asked 'now what?' He was feeling it too, in a big way.

"Do you want some sauce?" he asked after a few not-uncomfortably awkward seconds.

"That'd be great, thanks," Pixie said with a nod. "But that's not why I came here, I promise."

"It's fine if you did," Jude said, heading toward his fridge and the crowded rows of bottles he'd carefully arranged inside. He passed a full bottle over to Pixie and wondered why their conversation suddenly sounded and felt so normal. Maybe adjusting wouldn't be as hard as he thought. "Not like I'll run out of this stuff any time soon. Or if I do, you can always ask Eva."

"Cool," Pixie said after taking a long swig and wiping his mouth with the back of his hand. He shot Jude a smile, but seemed thoughtful, like he was also considering something new and unexpected. "You know what? I might be able to actually go in and have some there, in a restaurant, like an actual normal person. That's kind of amazing."

"You mean, you've never…" Jude stopped as Pixie's smile started to fade. "No, I guess you wouldn't."

Pixie shrugged. "It's not a big deal. It's just that there's people there, you know? It's hard to be around people when you got something heavy going on." He took another sip, smaller this time, but still clearly enjoying it. "But like I said, it's no biggie. There aren't a whole lot of people I actually want to hang out with, or who I'd know how to talk to, so. Not like I'm missing much, right?"

"You still want to, though," Jude said, feeling his way forward like inching across a fragile, fire-weakened floor. "Even if nobody really understands, sometimes it's better than being alone. It's easy to get… lost in yourself, if that makes sense."

"Sure does." Pixie was watching him now, as carefully as Jude was considering his own words. But the edge of apprehension was gone. They weren't circling each other at arm's length anymore, they were meeting each other halfway.

"Nice scarf," Jude said, nodding at the new red fabric loosely tied around Pixie's neck. It hid the awful scars just as well, but now Jude would never be able to look at it without remembering what lay beneath.

"What, this old thing?" Pixie grinned and played with the folds, moving his head so the shiny silk caught the light better. "It's Jasper's. He said I wore it better, but I dunno, you've seen some of his outfits, right? Awesome."

"I thought it looked familiar," Jude said with a rare smile, finally recalling the last time he'd seen it on its previous owner. It had only been a few days ago, but it felt like a lifetime. "It looks nice."

"Thanks. Also," Pixie continued, a note of anxiety entering his voice. "Um, thanks for... you know, back there, when I was, uh, not doing great? You covered it up." He waved one hand at his newly-decorated neck, an airy motion, like it was no big deal, but the lightness didn't come close to reaching his troubled eyes. "I was super out of it, but I remember that, I really don't like people seeing it that much, and just, I appreciate it, so, thanks."

"It was nothing. You would have done the same for me." Jude believed that with all his heart. He couldn't imagine saying that when this had all began, but then, he'd seen and done a lot of things he'd never imagined possible. "You don't have to answer, but... did Cruce...?"

"No," Pixie said, gaze dropping to the floor. He seemed to shrink down into himself a bit, and Jude immediately inwardly kicked himself for whatever painful memory his question had set off. "No, he's not the one who... it was someone else."

"Someone else," Jude repeated, remembering Cruce's cryptic words, hints at a 'master,' who'd given him specific orders. Orders involving Pixie. Most likely from the same 'someone else' at whom Pixie had hinted before. The one who'd killed him. Brutally. With their teeth. A chill swept over Jude. "Are they going to be a problem?"

"Probably," Pixie said, voice as faint as it had been when he'd lay helpless in Jude's arms down in the cave. "He's... not a good guy. I don't, um—thinking about him is kind of hard. Can we...?"

"Later. Don't worry," Jude said, and he could see the tension drain from Pixie's shoulders, the fear fade from his face. "We'll worry about all that later. And I'll be here." He meant every word, and didn't regret regret a thing.

Slowly, Pixie looked up, met his eyes, and smiled. Something deep in Jude's chest felt warm. "Thank you."

Maybe it was a mistake, promising protection to a vampire. But, again, Jude knew if their positions were reversed, Pixie would stand right with him through it all. And it made what he had to say next even harder. He stayed quiet for a moment, evaluating risks, calculating odds. The next step was the biggest yet, but it was safe. He knew that like he knew how to find solid ground that wouldn't collapse under his feet. "Pixie?"

"Yeah?" his voice was tight as well, and his eyes were locked on Jude's. He could clearly tell Jude was gearing up for something significant, and he was right there with him. If they fell, they fell together.

"There's something I learned a long time ago. When you walk through fire with someone," Jude started slowly. "Which I feel like we did…"

"Fire, really?" Pixie grinned, picking up where Jude trailed off. The change in subject seemed to relax him, however anxious the two of them still were. His laugh was nervous, but it was still an improvement. "I must have been unconscious for that part."

"It's a metaphor—this time." Jude shot Pixie a look, but not a genuinely annoyed one. "And I'm serious."

"I'm listening," Pixie reassured him. There was a slight giggle in his voice, but his expression soon reverted to the mixture of nervousness and hope Jude understood so well by now. "Go ahead."

"Anyway," Jude continued, but dropped his eyes to the floor, unable to watch Pixie's face as he spoke. "Going through that has a way of tying you together. When you find someone you trust enough who'll walk through the fire right along with you, you don't ever really want to face it without that person again."

"And that's me?" Pixie's voice sounded almost shy, as terrifyingly vulnerable as Jude felt, and he made himself look back up, surprised to find a smile on his face. Faint, fragile, but real.

"I have a lot of pieces to put back together," Jude said. "Me and Eva, me and Jasper. Felix. And I don't know what comes next. But feeling like this has to mean something. This has to be worth hanging onto. Whatever comes, I want to face it with you."

"Even the parts with Jasper and Felix?" Pixie's tone was a little dry, and his expression a lot knowing.

"What?" Jude could feel his face flushing again. The way Pixie tilted his head and grinned didn't help.

"Come on."

"You can tell," he said with a sigh, resigned. Anything else was a losing battle, one Jude was fine with surrendering.

"Everybody can tell. Everybody living or dead can tell. People who aren't living or dead could probably—"

"Yes, I get the picture," Jude said, the heat in his face not dying down a single degree. "And yes. Jasper and Felix and I, before any of this—five years ago—we were heading some kind of direction. I think. I'm not even sure where, but…"

"Uh-huh." Pixie said with a satisfied nod, as if he knew exactly which direction.

"It's not what you're thinking." Jude didn't know if his sudden defensiveness was because of discussing a hard-to-navigate situation with a relatively new person, or just his desire to mentally backflip away from hard-to-navigate situations in general. "Even if I care about them, and want—something, I'm not really someone who…" He stopped, suddenly more afraid to continue here than he would be walking into a burning building. Some things never got easier, not when you were talking about them with someone whose opinion actually mattered. "People getting together and falling in love—romantic love, anyway? And having sex or anything else? It's not something I ever had much interest in."

"Aro-ace?"

"I think grey on both." The moment the words left his mouth, his eyes went to the unnaturally pale pallor of Pixie's cheeks, and his own cheeks flushed even hotter. "I mean, a different kind of grey. No offense."

"None taken." Jude was sure Pixie was trying not to laugh now—and for once, he didn't mind.

Jude almost laughed himself. "My point is, before any of this, at least I had a good handle on who I was. It took me a long time to get there. Then I met Eva—and she's like me, she gets it. She gets me. But I never expected to… I just never expected Jasper and Felix, that's all. I was never really sure what to make of them—I'm still not!" He smiled again, but it faded quickly. "We never got the chance to figure it out for sure. And I didn't think it would ever…come up again. But it did." He said the last three words looking directly into Pixie's eyes, praying for him to understand the words Jude found so challenging to speak, harder than facing any nightmare.

"This stuff can be confusing as hell," Pixie said, still in a much lighter tone than Jude would have expected. He relaxed, just a fraction. "Way worse than growing fangs—that's easy, I'm a vampire, *I vant blood,* no questions there. But figuring anything else out is weird and messy and some people never get it down a hundred percent. But it's all cool."

"I know. But now it's even more confusing," Jude said a little more slowly than before, finding it hard to keep looking into Pixie's eyes. "I didn't expect them. And I definitely didn't expect you. But having you here…"

"I'm definitely here." Again, completely relaxed. Jude envied Pixie's calm as much as he appreciated it. "If you want me to be."

"I do," Jude said, this time without hesitation. "But the rest of it—it's going to take us a while to figure it out. Any of it. It's an adjustment. Especially for Felix." Jude fell silent for a moment, feeling hollow. "I can't even imagine what it was like. How do you come back from that?"

"It's hard." Pixie spoke slowly, one thumb carefully passing over the scarring on the back of one hand. "Really… really hard. It's not something you forget, that's for sure. But he was down there for years, I was just a few days, maybe a week, tops, when I first got turned, and this last time combined. So it's not like I'd… know…"

Pixie stopped, and his eyes slipped slightly out of focus. Something like fear passed over his face, and his pierced-and-healed hands began to shake. Slowly, praying he was doing the right thing, Jude reached out and gently took one of Pixie's hands in his. As he'd noticed before, the vampire's skin wasn't cold or clammy. Aside from the grey coloration, it felt like holding any other human's hand—except that this hand, unlike most other humans', was one

Jude actually enjoyed touching. And, from the way Pixie looked up at him, looking surprised as expected but eyes lit up with happiness instead of fear, the feeling had to be mutual.

"Yes you would," Jude said in a low voice. "This isn't a contest. If it was, we'd all lose, because there's no winning in going through Hell and back."

"Well, I think we'd all win." The corner of Pixie's mouth curled, but Jude couldn't tell if it was a smile or a grimace. "I think you kind of automatically win just for surviving. But I guess that's easier said than done."

"You did survive," Jude said firmly as Pixie's eyes dropped again. "If there's one thing I know, it's that surviving and living aren't the same thing. You can survive and not live. I did that for five years. But you're still here, the most *alive* person I've ever known. Your life still counts. It's proof that some things, even death can't take away."

"Like you said," Pixie said quietly, looking down at their joined hands. "Some things are worth hanging onto."

"Just to be entirely clear," Jude asked, hating to break the moment but terrified of misstepping after coming so far. "We are talking about… you and me… being together?"

"If we're not," Pixie said, lifting up their hands and giving Jude's a slight squeeze. "Then one of us is really confused here. And it would be me. Because yeah, that's definitely what I'm talking about!"

"Okay. Good. Me too." All at once, he felt hyperaware of every inch of his person, his tingling skin, his suddenly-unsteady legs and the mercifully faint but familiar phantom-limb sensation that made up the background of his life, now and maybe forever. Of the cool, soft breeze from the open, badly-repaired window. Of Pixie's surprisingly warm hand in his, and how very close they were standing. He was well used to the distortions of time after trauma, how days seemed like years, years seemed like hours. He wasn't used to actually wanting moments to last forever.

"So," Pixie said at last, breaking the spell in a way Jude didn't mind at all. "Does this mean I can use the window whenever I want?"

Jude's cheeks ached. When had he started smiling? When had Pixie gotten so firmly under his skin, become such a part of his life it felt like he had always been here? "You can even use the door."

Pixie let his head drop, giving a soft laugh. Then he looked up, raising his eyebrows in an expectant way. "Jude?"

"Yeah?"

"Are you *ever* going to kiss me?"

"I was getting there," Jude said, mouth dry and hands sweaty, shaking and overjoyed and terrified in the best way. "If that's all right."

"Oh yeah," Pixie said, smiling as he leaned forward. "You are so invited."

Nothing in the past few days had been what Jude expected, and this was no different. Vampires were supposed to be terrifying, lethal, predatory monsters, sharp-fanged and bloodthirsty. Everything about Pixie was soft and warm in Jude's arms, and so were his lips. Even the small points of his fangs weren't painfully sharp, would never be. He sighed into the kiss like he was slipping into a warm bath after the longest night of his life, and Jude felt every aching muscle in his own body relax into a peace he hadn't known for five very long years, if not longer. When Jude pulled him close to sink down together onto his battered couch, it felt like coming home. The night wasn't deadly, the shadows weren't threatening, and Pixie didn't taste like death. Far from it.

Hot, spicy steak sauce, like kissing vampires, was an acquired taste. But nothing was sharp here, or cold, or missing. Nothing hurt. For the first time in so long, they were alive. And with every passing moment, Jude acquired more of a taste for both.

🔥

The next day, Eva felt almost normal. 'Almost' because her definition of normal tended to involve more exhaustion and stress than others' and, today, she felt rested, relaxed, and somehow reset. New page, new game. Nothing was going to throw her for a loop today, she thought—not even The Pit's door flying open as soon as she got close. She jumped back, narrowly avoiding another blow to her still-sore nose. At least she didn't have coffee this time.

"Whoop, sorry!" said the short girl who shot out the door, stopping just before barreling into Eva. She had also-short, spiky blonde hair and carried an umbrella in one hand, a takeout box with a familiar red logo in the other. She wore long sleeves and gloves despite the warm day, and her face had an odd, grey cast to it—but that might have just been the umbrella's shadow. "I mean, excuse me."

She held the door with her foot as another girl came out, also carrying a takeout box and umbrella. This one wore a t-shirt over her long sleeves, bright red and reading *We'll Meet You in The Pit!* She was much taller and a darker shade of grey. The smile she shot Eva flashed by quickly, too fast for Eva to be sure if the points to her teeth were real or imagined. "Have a great day!"

Before Eva could answer, they were gone, sprinting away across the polished mall floor. Eva opened her mouth, ready to call *no running* after the fast-disappearing teenagers, but thought better of it, shaking her head. For once, she'd take the advice she'd given to Jude, who should be back on duty today. Sometimes, she didn't have to carry the world on her shoulders. Somewhat startled, but regaining composure fast, Eva headed into the restaurant and its relative quiet.

The Pit was an oasis of low lighting and music—some kind of freeform jazz, which Eva had never especially enjoyed, but had to admit fit in here. According to Magnolia, the place was just starting to catch on, and soon they might actually turn a profit. Starting up a restaurant in this God-awful economy (she'd been known to say to anyone who'd listen) would have been a mistake for most people, but not them. The place was Dorian's brainchild. While she oversaw management and finances, he had free reign to experiment with meats and spices, blood-infused sauces, and other things Eva hadn't really paid much attention to until they became personally relevant. She had to admit, judging from the ambience to the wafting savory smells, they'd pulled it together pretty well.

Eva could count the number of times she'd actually been inside on one hand, though now seemed to be a good time, in the lull before the lunchtime rush. Only a few people sat scattered at small tables-for-one, or at the bar. One large corner booth, however, was occupied by a single woman. She didn't look up, seeming focused on shuffling a deck of cards, but Eva had the immediate feeling that she was aware of everything in the restaurant, including her.

"I see you met the new delivery girls," she said as Eva approached. She never looked up, or stopped shuffling her cards, but a smirk pulled at the corner of her mouth. "They're a little over-enthusiastic, but I think it'll be a good fit."

"Were they..." Eva started, pointing her thumb over her shoulder and throwing the door a glance, before shaking her head. "Never mind. Hi, I'm Eva. Heard you were a big help to some of my friends a few nights ago."

"Letizia," she answered, shooting her a quick glance as she shuffled. How many times had Eva walked by her doing exactly this outside Jasper's store? They'd exchanged nods on a few occasions but never words. Odd to think that so much strangeness and truth was there all the time, never far away. "And it was my pleasure entirely. I've been waiting a long time to take out that particular trash."

"Almost makes me wish I'd been there," Eva said, remembering Felix's haunted eyes and burned palms, the way Jude's face went even paler than usual when he tried to talk about anything she'd missed. "Almost."

"And what about now? Seeking answers?"

"Not so much," Eva said, sliding into the booth across from her new acquaintance. "If you'd asked me that a few days ago, I would've said something different. But now I've got about all the answers I can stand. I mean, vampires?" She gave a short, bemused laugh. "No offense, but you're a little out of my frame of reference. What am I supposed to do with that information?"

"It was a shock for me too," Letizia said, sounding a little more thoughtful than her customary quips. "But you get used to it."

"Do you mean just *knowing* about it," Eva asked carefully, lowering her voice. "Or actually... *being* one?"

"Both." Letizia stopped shuffling and set her cards down in a perfectly aligned stack. "All of this 'information' was as unbelievable and terrifying a century and a half ago as it is now. Maybe more."

"Yeah, where did you say you were from, Venice?" Eva suppressed a sympathetic grimace. "Kind of Church Central, right? Especially a hundred or so years ago."

"Some things never change, even if we do." Letizia flashed her pointed teeth in a tight smile. She lay three cards facedown in a line on the table between them. "The Church still breathes down peoples' necks, but at least here they do it from a distance. Fortunately, I wasn't left to figure everything out on my own. And neither, it seems, are you."

"Yeah..." Eva leaned back, crossing her arms. "Even if it seems like everyone else kinda got a head start. Not sure how I feel about that yet, even if it's half my own damn fault. Jude tried to tell me a million times and I wouldn't hear it."

"Seeing is believing, as they say." Letizia seemed to regard Eva with the same mixture of curiosity and slight apprehension, tempered with the same desire to trust. "Skepticism is healthy for things you can't see—but those things have a way of turning too real to ignore."

"You got that right." Eva murmured as Letizia flipped one of the cards face-up. Eva looked down at the brightly-painted yellow sunlight and rainbow of flowers. A small, happy-looking figure danced through a meadow, followed by a small white dog.

"The Fool," she read from the scrawled text across the top of the card, wrinkling her nose. "I've sure felt like one lately."

"Not that kind of fool," Letizia said with a one-shoulder shrug. "This one means a new beginning—the start of a journey. But a happy one. The future is bright and it's not a journey you'll have to take alone."

"Yeah, that's been one of the only good things about the past five years," Eva reflected. "Having your lives wrecked can kind of bring you closer together while you try to pick up the pieces."

"But...?" Letizia raised one angular eyebrow; Eva's hesitation had been slight, but apparently not slight enough to miss.

"But, honestly, it's just nice to be around women!" Eva said with a laugh, feeling her cheeks heat up. Don't get me wrong, some of my best friends are men, but..."

When she trailed off, Letizia gave her a crooked smile that prompted her to continue. "But sometimes you need a break?"

Eva nodded and tried to clamp down on her giggles, some of the tension easing from her shoulders. "See, you know. I mean, it's incredible having Felix back. Beyond incredible, we missed him so much. And I'm sure Pixie's great too, I'm looking forward to meeting him. But now the boys are going all soul-searching and 'what are we,' and I don't really... have anything to add here, you know? I wouldn't know sexual attraction if it bit me—no offense."

Letizia grinned wider than her usual closed-mouth smile, and Eva caught a flash of fangs, fighting down her startle reflex. Even bared in a smile instead of a snarl, those things took some getting used to. "None taken."

"It's always been easier being around Jude," Eva continued, feeling a little more comfortable with every word. "But now he's all caught up in the attraction mess too—which has gotta be weird for him..."

"Weird for everyone, I'd imagine." Despite her dry, understated tone, Letizia still seemed amused, or maybe just happy. Maybe this was as refreshing (and complicated) conversation for her as it was for Eva. "And don't worry, I know about attraction spectrums and orientations, gender spectrums too—you don't need to explain."

"Huh, really?" Eva blinked. For some reason she hadn't expected a vampire from the 19th century to be acquainted with what most people considered a relatively recent development—or an internet-based invention, she thought with slight bitterness. "That's…refreshing."

"These things have been around a lot longer than I have," Letizia said, seemingly in response to Eva's thoughts. "And I've been around a while. But I understand, it takes less energy to be around people who understand you—who, as I said, you don't need to explain yourself to. And sometimes it's easier to be alone." She was quiet for a moment. "My 'break' has been one-hundred-fifty years and counting."

"That's quite a break," Eva said, shaking her head. Maybe someday her rational brain would stop rebelling whenever someone casually dropped something vampire-flavored into a conversation, but it wouldn't be today. "Ever miss 'em?"

"One or two." Letizia's smile faded, and for a split-second, she looked unspeakably sad. But the moment passed, and her smile came back fast. "But I get a lot done."

Letizia flipped the second card and almost dropped it. She raised her eyebrows and gave a slight, surprised-sounding 'hm!', before setting the card down the way it had turned in her hand—sideways, perpendicular to the first. This one had a lion with a red-gold mane that looked like flames and on its back rode a victorious-looking figure with two raised fists.

"So what's that one mean?" Eva asked, though the image was triumphant enough for her to make an educated guest.

"Strength," Letizia said. "And it means exactly that. The drive to persevere, rallying one's forces—or friends—and bending a situation to your will. Reversed, it would mean a collapse, a breakdown of defenses or resources, hitting a brick wall."

"Ouch," Eva winced, wishing the description didn't feel quite so familiar. "So which is it?"

Letizia tilted her head to look at the sideways card. "Neither. It's lying down—Strength is taking a break. Even lionesses need a nap sometimes."

"All right, point taken." Eva stretched her legs out under the table, easing into a more relaxed position. It was amazing how every muscle wanted to clench if she wasn't actively trying to relax them. They sat in a surprisingly comfortable silence for a few seconds before Eva spoke again. "Come here often?"

"The mall, or here in particular?"

"The Pit. It's my sister's, but I can't remember the last time I actually came in here," Eva's eyebrows came together as she realized. "I guess it's like living in New York but never visiting the Statue of Liberty. You know it's there, but don't really go out of your way."

"I'm in here every couple weeks, when my supplies run low," Letizia said. She spoke casually where Eva was still fighting the urge to lower her voice when anything even remotely *related* came up. "The Pit and Jasper's shop are about the closest I come to regular haunts."

"What about The Abyss?" Eva couldn't help but imagine Letizia in the middle of a sea of teenagers wearing spiked bracelets and colorful, just-as-spiky hair.

"I think I scare most of the clientele," the witch said with a droll smile. "But it's fun to visit."

"So, if you're in here all the time, does that mean they know…?" Eva shot a look toward the kitchen, as if expecting Magnolia or Dorian to come out any minute, zero in on her, and telepathically know all the weirdness of the past few days. "We obviously haven't talked about anything."

"I'm just a barbecue aficionado," Letizia said. Through almost the entire conversation, she'd had a slight smile that suggested it was all a game. Their secrets were potentially deadly, but somehow she made them seem almost fun. Eva wondered if she'd ever reach that point, hoped she did. "And this place has the best sauce in town."

"I'll tell Mags you said that next time I see her," Eva said. "And I'll grab some while I'm here. I gave Jude enough to last a year, but that was before, uh… life got interesting."

"Too interesting?"

"After my old job, I was looking forward to a little boredom," Eva admitted with a smaller pang than she would have expected. "But it looks like that's just not in the cards, is it?"

Instead of answering, Letizia turned over the last card. Lovers embraced against a backdrop of flowers and stars. "They usually have a plan of their own."

Spread apparently done, she swept her cards together and moved to slip them all back into the deck. But as she touched the last card, the Lovers, another card slipped from the rest, and fell right on top of it, perpendicular. Letizia stared down at it, her brow slowly furrowing, until Eva could tell she was glaring at it from behind her dark sunglasses, apparently not at all liking what she saw.

"What is it?" Eva leaned forward, tilting her head to look at the sideways card. She saw the flames first. They surrounded a monstrous face, all sharp teeth and twisting horns, eyes shining metallic and gold-leaf bright. Across the bottom was the Roman numeral for fifteen, XV, and two words Eva read out loud. "The Devil."

"Yes, he is," Letizia murmured, leaning back in her seat to gaze down at the cards, tapping a sharp fingernail against the rest of her gathered deck. "And yes, they do have a plan. They certainly do. Some things you can't stop coming, no matter how you try to break the circle. It always comes back around."

"What plan?" Eva asked, a chill racing down her spine and arms. Her hair was standing on end, she could feel it, like there was a static electricity in the air. The moment before a lightning strike. "What's coming?"

The Witch's black lip curled up in a crooked smile, but it wasn't a happy one. Behind it, one sharp fang gleamed, bright as the Devil's eyes. When she spoke, Eva didn't understand her meaning, but the words made her shiver all the more.

"The sweet darkness, and the wicked gold."

It was a late overcast afternoon, not a full moon night. The sun was setting, and the low-hanging clouds had cleared barely enough to let a few stray beams through, yellow-orange and darkening as night neared.

No waves crashed against a white beach. No terrified cries echoed, no fires blazed. No burned figure washed up on the sand, no mask.

But the stone circle remained.

Sharp points of black crystal thrust toward the slate-grey clouds and patches of dying sunlight. As if they'd always been there, in the middle of a park in the heart of a major city, instead of a world only glimpsed in dreams, after hearts stopped beating and screams fell silent.

As it had been for years, the ring of stones was perfectly quiet and still, as were the trees surrounding it, as if the urban woods themselves feared interrupting a sacred silence. But no silence lasted forever. Eventually, in this place where time seemed suspended, frozen in a single undying moment, there came a small change, without warning or explanation.

A crack appeared in one of the onyx spires, interrupting its smooth, glossy surface. From it fell a small piece, like cut glass—which stopped in midair, inches before it hit the ground, pointed end down and spinning like a top.

The shard continued to spin, hovering for several seconds, glittering gold in the dwindling sunset.

Finally, when the last of the day's fading light was gone, it stopped and fell.

Acknowledgments

Thank you so much to Moo and Kevie for supporting, feeding, and loving me while I worked on this weird book.

Thank you to Noel Arthur Hemipel for the use of the amazing Numinous Tarot images! I can't wait to get my hands on the real thing. ♥

Thank you to the Kraken Collective for being awesome and helping make *Stake Sauce* as gorgeous (and coherent) as possible, particularly Lyssa Chiavari's dynamite graphic design, and Claudie Arseneault's always-magical editing wizardry.

Thank you to Eri for listening to me babble endlessly about these dork vampires, and babbling back until it turned into something super freaking awesome. If I do say so.

And thank you to everyone who's followed me since *Chameleon Moon*—I hope you like this just as much, and find it fun, exciting, and validating to read. I certainly did.

About The Author

RoAnna Sylver is passionate about stories that give hope, healing and even fun for LGBT, disabled and other marginalized people, and thinks we need a lot more.

Aside from writing oddly optimistic dystopia books, RoAnna is a blogger, artist, singer and voice actor, is an actual genetic mutant (and proud), knows too much about Star Trek, and lives with family and a small snorking dog near Portland, OR.

The next adventure RoAnna would like is a nap in a pile of bunnies.

Also By the Author

THE CHAMELEON MOON SERIES

Chameleon Moon
The Lifeline Signal
Life Within Parole

MODULATING FREQUENCIES

Stake Sauce
Death Masquerade

Printed in Great Britain
by Amazon